SILVER TRACK

Having travelled to a wild frontier town in search of answers about his brother's death, Ben Jody finds himself not only in the middle of a bitter conflict between rival railroad companies, but also accused by the Army of being a deserter. With his good name tarnished and the law hot on his heels, he has little choice but to run. On discovering who is responsible for his brother's death though, Ben decides to ride right into the face of danger . . .

CALEB RAND

SILVER TRACK

Complete and Unabridged

LINFORD
Leicester

First published in Great Britain in 2012 by
Robert Hale Limited
London

First Linford Edition
published 2013
by arrangement with
Robert Hale Limited
London

A catalogue record for this book is available
from the British Library.

ISBN 978–1–4448–1707–2

Published by
F. A. Thorpe (Publishing)
Anstey, Leicestershire

1

The powerful lamp of the Twin Rivers locomotive beamed its light through the late spring snowfall as the watchman stepped from Duckwater's waiting room. There was a muffled hiss of steam and a squeal of brakes as the five-car train slid to a stop alongside the platform.

'Move along there,' the Yellowstone watchman called out, edging away from the lee of the clapboards.

Near the step of the first coach, a tall man, who was wearing a wolf-skin coat and carrying a canvas grip, looked about cheerlessly. 'Oh, you're talking to me,' Ben Jody countered. 'Sorry, it sounded like you were scaring off some mangy dog.' He moved on, but after a couple of paces turned back. 'Can I get up to Harpers Gap, tonight?' he asked.

The watchman adjusted the shotgun in the crook of his arm. Then he moved into the open and shook his head. 'Try the stage,' he suggested bluntly.

'How long does that take?'

'You'll have to ask *them*,' he responded with a shrug.

The station's cheerless waiting room had a puncheon floor and was edged by plain benches. A pot-bellied stove leaked feeble heat and the frosty air was laced with stale tobacco and coal smoke.

Ben stepped up to the ticket window. 'Anything going to Harpers Gap?' he asked the ticket agent.

'If it ain't closed, there might be a constructor's car goin' up there.' The agent was already turning away when Ben continued.

'Can the stage make it?' he asked.

'There's no tellin'. In this weather, one day they run, next day they don't.'

'Is there an office?'

'Yeah. It's out o' here, an' down the street. You can't miss it,' the man said, then tilted his head to the click of the telegraph key.

'Is there somewhere I could hire a

horse? The livery stable, maybe?' Ben persisted.

The agent eyed Ben speculatively. 'No one's goin' to hire or sell anythin' until this blow's over,' he said. 'You must want to get there real bad.'

Ben didn't answer, but took a long, low disappointed breath.

The agent looked up as the waiting room's door opened. 'Willis,' he said. 'There's somethin' here for the general. Take it over to him, will you?'

'You've got a general in town?' Ben queried with what sounded like casual, time-killing interest.

'General Ambrose Quill. He's president o' this Twin Rivers stretch o' railroad,' the agent replied. 'That's his car in the sidin'.'

'I used to know an Ambrose Quill,' Ben said. 'It was some time ago, but there can't be more than one with a handle like that.'

He turned from the ticket window and went out through the near door, was back on the platform before

3

realizing it wasn't the way out to the street.

It was nearing full dark now, and the Yellowstone guard was still on duty. The man's challenging glance told Ben that it would be for the best if he moved on. As he reached for the door to go back, he could see the double grooves where the line of the siding track ran. The lights of the private coach glowed temptingly through the wintry gloom, and he half smiled. *Ambrose Quill, eh?* he thought to himself.

For a moment, the thought awakened a distant memory in Ben. He saw hazy images of troopers and campfires, a figure on an iron grey horse, heard the affecting notes of a bugle recalling a cavalry charge. He shivered, cursed as he looked back at the watchman.

'I'm making a call on the general. Do I go alone, or are you escorting me?' he asked. With the toe of his boot, he pushed his grip against the low wall. They left the shelter of the station and started on up the platform. The wind chilled them, but for Ben there was suddenly an added sensation. 'Do you take such an interest in every passenger that alights here, or is this personal?' he shouted almost cheerfully over the bite of the wind.

'It's a job,' the watchman gruffed. 'Yesterday the Twin Rivers Railroad paid me. Today the Yellowstone are payin' me a bit more.'

The two men trudged silently past a water tank that was shrouded in swirling snow, then they stepped over to the siding. A few feet above their heads, the lights of the private rail car intensified against the blackness. At the foot of the rear steps, the guard told Ben to wait up. He climbed to the platform and rapped loudly on the door.

'Evenin', Mister Paynter,' the guard said, as the door swung open. 'There's a feller here, wants to see the general.'

'Who shall I say?' Paynter queried brusquely.

'Say it's a boy from Missionary Ridge. That should be enough,' Ben answered back. As the railroad engineer stepped onto the platform to peer down at him, Ben was thinking the man's name was also one he recognized.

Paynter's face broke from what looked like a harried look to a thin smile. 'He'll always see an ol' rebel biter. In fact, he'll . . . ' His words broke off when a hefty man in a flared overcoat, suddenly pushed out from the car.

'I'll be in touch,' the man said, as he swung lithely down the steps.

Paynter grunted an unintelligible response, stood watching until the man's frame melted into the snowy darkness. Then, he looked down at Ben.

'Stand there much longer, and you'll set solid. Come on up,' he said.

As he passed the Yellowstone guard, Ben glanced at him and winked. 'They don't pay you half enough,' he said, but didn't think the man saw or heard him.

He had a quick look at the handsome furnishings as he followed Paynter inside the car. But his eyes were always making towards the slight figure who sat behind the highly polished desk. It was Ambrose Quill all right. The years had aged him some, but there was no doubt Ben was confronting the man he'd thought to be one of the greatest field commanders to make it through the war.

The impersonal, questioning look that Ambrose Quill had focused on Ben, tempered slightly. He came out from behind the desk and extended his hand. 'Don't hold it against me if I don't recognize you, soldier. Missionary Ridge was a somewhat misty day, I recall.'

'Yes, we were up in the clouds,' Ben replied. 'The name's Jody, sir. Benedict Jody.'

The general smiled comfortably and indicated one of his overstuffed chairs.

'What do you think's going to happen with Poole?' Sam Paynter asked as Ben was shedding his coat.

Not knowing, Quill shook his head. 'God knows.'

Paynter thought something for a moment. 'Then I'll say good night, gentlemen,' he said instead, picked up his own coat and hat and left.

The general sat back down at his desk, looked across at Ben. 'All we've got to do is lay track up to Windhammer. Huh, you'd think rational men could find a way to do that, wouldn't you? I suppose you've heard of the problem we've got?' he asked.

Ben suddenly realized what the ticket agent had meant about the constructor's car. Windhammer was across the Musselshell, nearly fifty miles beyond Harpers Gap. He shook his head innocently. 'No sir, can't say I have,' he admitted. 'I just heard you're the boss. The president of this section of railroad.'

'Yeah I'm that all right,' Quill said. 'Unfortunately, it doesn't mean folk stand back and salute as we build the track. Are you taking some sort of furlough, Jody?'

'Not quite, sir. I resigned my commission.'

'You were an officer?'

'Captain. Brigadier Bonnie's cavalry.

Right now, I'm on my way up to Harpers Gap. I heard you were here, and thought I'd pay my respects,' Ben said and smiled.

'Noel Bonnie's a fine man . . . tolerant too,' Quill said reacting to Ben's resignation from the Federal Army.

'Yes sir. And just as well, seeing as I'm soon to marry his daughter.'

'Well, what do you know?' Quill chuckled and opened his hands in surprise. 'I've probably met the girl. I guess she'd have been no more than a button.'

'Maybe an inch or two more than that, sir. It sure is a small world, though,' Ben offered.

'That usually depends on what standpoint you've got,' Quill observed dryly. 'Look, Jody, Harpers Gap is more or less our operations centre,' he continued. 'If that's where you're headed, why not work for us? Unless you've something already lined up, that is.'

'I do, General,' Ben replied. 'Besides, I know nothing of railroads.'

Quill nodded understandingly. 'I

realize that,' he said. 'Why don't you find out what I've got in mind. You're not going anywhere just yet.'

'That's true enough,' Ben agreed. 'Won't do any harm, I guess.'

Quill nodded his satisfaction. He got up from his desk to open a door in the rear corner of the car. 'Ralph. Could you come in here?' he called.

Ben got to his feet as a man wearing garters around the sleeves of his shirt, appeared in the doorway.

'Captain Jody, this is Ralph Curtin, one of our engineers,' Quill introduced the man. 'He'll explain what I have in mind. Play your cards right, and he'll pour you some civilized coffee,' he added.

'We'll go to my office,' Curtin said, indicating that Ben go ahead along the corridor to the room at the far end of the rail car.

The room contained a high slanting drawing-table with a green-shaded lamp above, a suite of plans chests and a pair of straight-backed chairs.

'You want me to draw railways?' Ben

asked with a smile.

'Hah, no. That's what I do. We want you to do something far more exciting. Far better paid, too.'

'Better tell me then,' Ben said, as Curtin stepped forward to look out a mug for the coffee.

'Well, we've been having trouble procuring ties,' the engineer started. 'Someone's been giving back-handers to see that our orders aren't being filled. It's on track now — so to speak — but they'll start again. And when that happens, we can't lay iron. We want to know who's behind it.'

'Yes, I see that. But I'm an ex-cavalry captain, not one of them Pinkerton fellers.'

'The person we send up there's got to be a stranger, and reliable. General Quill obviously reckons you're both . . . worth the two hundred bucks a month that goes with it.'

'That's all I'd have to do? Let you know what's going on?'

'Not me . . . Sam Paynter. You'd

11

probably have to loosen a few tongues with whiskey sweeteners. They'll be for Royston Poole's crew.'

'Who's he?' Ben queried.

'The son-of-a-bitch we were forced to sign a new tie contract with. Right now he's directing operations, and if he doesn't deliver, we stop laying iron.'

'I see. Was that him leaving when I arrived? Big feller?'

'Yeah, could've been. They were wanting to see him. Why?'

'No reason ... heard someone mention his name. So, if you could find this reliable stranger, when would you expect him to start?' Ben asked with a wily look.

'Straightaway. I'd order the construc- tors' train up.'

'And it's bound for Harpers Gap?'

'It doesn't have much choice,' Curtin answered with an amused nod.

'Then you've just found who you're looking for,' Ben decided as he pulled on his coat. 'I'd best go and pick up my gear.'

2

It was a five-car train, three flatcars loaded with rails, one unheated coach and a caboose. As soon as Ben was aboard, it pulled in from the siding, stopped at the station to take on a full gang of navvies.

As the train hissed and chugged itself into motion, a burly, unshaven man in a blanket coat elbowed his way through the crowded gangway until he was two seats in front of Ben.

'Up you get, feller,' he snarled at a slight, wirily built man who was sitting nearest the aisle.

'Why? I got a ticket,' the man answered back, and Ben gave the thin smile of someone who knows a mistake's just been made.

The face of the burly man took on a broad, keen grin. 'Good for you,' he drawled, reaching down to clamp two hands on the seated man's coat lapels. With little effort, he lifted him to his feet and swung him up and out into the aisle. 'Use it to stand there,' he added. Then he took the seat himself, sprawled low, and pulled his hat down over his face.

'One day he'll try that on someone who don't want to move,' the man next to Ben muttered to no one in particular. But Ben had already lost interest. He dipped his head against the glare of the overhead lamps and closed his eyes.

Several times as the train ran on through the night he dozed. When he was awake, he overheard snatches of conversation, paid more attention than he normally would have, because now he was an employee of the Twin Rivers Railroad Company. On operational lease to the Yellowstone, Ambrose Quill was hoping to tap the riches of the Windhammer silver boom, use company money to build an extension through one of the high-country canyons. But the Yellowstone was building along the same route, employing everything from county politics and court fights to armed gangs, in contesting their right to lay track. It sounded to Ben as though Yellowstone had a claim on the Chisel Canyon where its main work camps were located. Twin Rivers had jumped to a point above what the men called 'Thousand Chains', and were already laying track along an upper rift of the Musselshell.

Apparently, a US State marshal had been hired by the Yellowstone to head up a dozen or more hardcases to intimidate any opposing force. Duckwater Station was little more than a company stronghold, and according to a tie hack sitting across the aisle from Ben, Harpers Gap was *an open wound, wrigglin' with pimps, coolies an' cappers.*

Ben had kept an eye open for Royston Poole, and at the Harpers Gap station as he was waiting to go down the platform steps, he saw him walk past in a crowd heading for the street. Ben thought, he'd probably ridden the caboose, gave him credit for having chosen a warm spot for the deeply uncomfortable, chilly trip.

★   ★   ★

Five miles north of Duckwater, they'd cleared the storm. Here, ankle-deep snow in the main street had already turned to slush. It was after full dark, but the town was still awake with steady traffic moving between the saloons. The men Ben passed didn't look like regular townsfolk. They were mostly armed, walked alone with drunken, unstable gaits.

To Ben's surprise, the lobby of the Full Board boarding house was clean and freshly painted, as was his room back along the hallway. He laid his grip on the bed, opened it long enough to take out two letters, a heavy shellbelt and a walnut-gripped .44 army revolver. He spent half a minute inspecting the pistol's action, making sure it carried a full load. Then he laid the fur coat aside and tucked the letters into an inside jacket pocket.

He left the room and went back along the hallway to the lobby, crossed to the desk at the head of the stairs.

'Can you tell me how I get to Doctor King's house?' he asked the clerk.

'Walk on up towards the river. Last house before you get to it.'

Ben half smiled, nodded his thanks.

'Lookin' for anyone in particular?' the man called after him.

Ben considered 'No, anyone will do,' as a deserving answer, but gave 'Yes, I am,' instead, and without stopping.

He walked the short distance to the end of the main street until he picked up the muted roar of the snow-melt that was flooding the Musselshell. Walking fast to warm himself against the sharp bite of the still air, he started wondering about Eady Bonnie, again. He was kindling a small hope that she wouldn't go on as he'd suggested, that she'd wait for him in Rock Springs. In Duckwater before the train loaded up,

17

he'd asked the telegraph agent to forward any messages for him. Whatever she decided, he knew he'd hear from her.

A few minutes later, and on the edge of town, instinct told him he'd reached the King house. He stopped, thought for a moment and took a look around him, then he opened the gate and started across the front yard. He knocked on the front door of the house and waited, kicked off the thick rinds of snow from his boots.

When the door swung open, it took him a moment to identify Royston Poole. Outlined by the pale lamplight at the end of a short run of hallway, he was of stockier and taller build than Ben had realized.

'I called to see Doctor King,' Ben said at the lack of response from the big man.

'He's not here. And at this time o' day, I'd be sayin' he wasn't, even if he were, if you get my drift,' Poole replied.

'Yes, sorry, I know it's late. But it is important I see him,' Ben persisted.

The hint of a smile touched Poole's strong, heavy features. 'And I'm sorry, because this time he really isn't with us. Hasn't been for two days.'

A shock ran through Ben at the realization of what Poole was saying. Surprise and a bitter disappointment prevented him knowing what to say next.

Poole seemed to sense this. 'So whatever it was, doesn't really matter. And as I said, it's late,' he added and began to close the door.

'Wait.' Ben reached out quickly and held the door open. 'What happened? It must have been very sudden.'

Poole drew back half a step, increased his pressure on the door. 'He was collecting herbs an' such from the high creeks,' he drawled. 'From the look of him, he must have woke a whole nest of moccasins.' The man paused momentarily before adding, 'It's only been a few hours since the funeral, so if you'll just let the household be . . . '

Bearing a potential association in mind, Ben didn't want to antagonize

19

Poole. He'd come for some answers, at least to ask some questions.

'Is there someone else I can talk to?' he asked.

'His daughter, but she's not seeing you or anyone tonight. I don't know what it is with you feller, but I advise you get the hell away from here for a few days,' Poole rasped in rising anger.

For the shortest moment, there was a grind to Ben's jaw. 'I realize that right now you've got some fancy door-stopping to do,' he started, 'but I've come too far to be told to come back in a few days. Just go and ask her, will you? Tell her it's something that shouldn't wait. My name's Jody.'

Poole snorted, shook his head and pushed the door that now had Ben's boot against it.

'Who is it, Roy?' a girl's voice then called out from a room off the hallway.

'Someone who's made a mistake with the address. They're just going,' Poole added in a lower, more urgent tone.

Ben meant what he'd said about not

being put off, but saw nothing in Poole's expression to give away the sudden move as he edged into the opening. Quickly, Poole reached out and pinned Ben back against the door frame with a solid, powerful hold. Ben was already expecting the swing of Poole's fist when a shadow blocked the light from the hall.

'What's going on?' the girl asked.

Poole moved his grip on Ben's arm, twisted him back into the doorway. 'There's a feller here thinks he's got business with your pa,' he replied. 'I've just explained that he doesn't.'

Ben half-turned to see a tall, slender girl standing at the far end of the hall. 'I know it's a bad time, but I haven't a lot of choice,' he said. 'Will you just hear what I've got to say?' he asked.

'Let him in,' she told Poole.

Ben edged past the big man, met a hostile glare with his own. 'A feller took hold of me like that near Missionary Ridge in '63. I had to shove a mortar spike into his belly to make him let go,' he said quietly.

3

Ben took off his hat and crossed the hall to the room beyond where the girl stood waiting for him. It was a dining room, and a shaded lamp cast a warm light across the furniture. A working sampler lay on the centre table, beyond stood an ornate stove with shiny brass fenders.

'I tried to keep him out,' Poole said as he followed Ben into the room. 'He wouldn't listen.'

Standing beside a rocking chair, Willow King was watching Ben. 'Actually, it was me said to let him in,' she answered back. 'So, what is the important matter you wanted to see my pa about?' she asked Ben.

'That was between him an' me, ma'am. But maybe now it should be between you and me,' he replied tellingly.

22

Ben saw the girl's paleness, her tiredness. Her few words had been direct but lifeless and there was a forlorn look in her dark eyes. Her raven hair was drawn tightly back from her face, and her dress was black, unrelieved by any adornment.

For the first time, the girl's eyes moved away from Ben to Poole. 'Thank you for calling by, Roy,' she told him somewhat cursorily.

'I think I'll hang around,' he returned.

The girl gave him the faintest of smiles, and shook her head. 'I'll be all right. Pa's business can't just stop. I'll see you in the morning.'

For a moment Poole stood with his own thoughts, then he lifted his hat and heavy coat from the back of a chair just inside the door. 'Yeah, there'll be stuff you need from town,' he accepted, ignoring Ben completely.

'I'll let you know what.' Now the girl had a faint smile as she added, 'Good night.'

Only when the door had closed in the hallway, did the girl turn to Ben. 'Perhaps you'd better tell me who you are, and what you wanted to see my father about,' she said.

'I'm Captain Benedict Jody,' Ben began, deciding it wasn't worth correcting himself. He took the letters from his coat pocket and handed one of them over. 'This letter from your father reached me five days ago. Please read it.'

The girl took a single sheet from the envelope and read it once, then again more carefully. 'I'm sorry, I don't understand,' she said looking up.

Ben had been watching her closely, and now as she spoke he let out a breath of disappointment. 'Jesse Chayne doesn't mean anything to you?'

'No, I don't think so. Should it?' she asked. 'Obviously, my father knew him.'

'Well yes, in a way he did,' Ben agreed. 'Frank was in business with a man named Harry Gedding. The Silver Track, they called it.'

24

'Have I seen rail wagons with that name?' the girl asked.

'Maybe. It is a freighting outfit. They've got a yard, somewhere called Swimfish.'

'I know of it. It's upriver, a small camp for the Twin Rivers company. But what's that got to do with my father?'

'According to him, there was an accident and Jesse was drowned,' Ben said. 'Do *you* recall anything of it?'

'An accident up here's not unusual or rare, Captain Jody. But unless it *was*, Pa wouldn't talk about it. It's not something medical men do, I believe.'

'That's just it. Jesse's case *was* unusual. So perhaps there *is* somethin' you saw or heard,' Ben suggested.

The girl reached over to turn down the smoking wick of the lamp that hung low above the table. 'Needs refilling,' she muttered, giving her a moment for thought. 'Can I ask what's pushing you on this?' she asked instead of answering direct.

'A couple of things. Jesse drowning

was pretty unlikely, and your pa says he wasn't so sure it was an accident,' Ben said, and held out the second envelope. 'Jesse wasn't one for putting pen to paper, but I had this from him two weeks ago. He says he's in some sort of trouble — that if anything happens, it's caught up with him. That's what he wanted me to know, nothing else. I'm real sorry to be calling on you with all this, but I don't have anything else to go on.'

'I think I understand, Captain, and I'm sorry. But I've already tried to tell you, this really isn't the best time.'

Ben knew she was right, that he should be taking his leave, pinching back his anger and frustration.

'I'll thank you anyway, Miss King, but I can't help thinking you don't want to help. Your father must have known I'd come in response to his letter.'

'Perhaps he did, Captain. But he didn't tell me about it, and that's the way it is. Are you questioning my word?' Her head came up quickly, eyes now showing anger along with the hurt. 'I hope I didn't ask Mr Poole to leave too early,' she warned.

'I beg your pardon,' he said stiffly, raised his hand in apology. 'But I've travelled from Rock Springs, and that's not exactly down the street. Perhaps there's a friend of your father's who might know something?'

'I don't know. I doubt it.' Then the girl gave him a curious, calculating glance. 'You're a very stubborn man, aren't you?'

'Not overly. Not enough to make me lose sight of the truth of what happened up here.'

As unmistakeable notice that Ben's time was finally up, she shook her head and turned away.

'Please accept my commiserations,' he said, walking to the door. 'I wish the circumstances could be different for you and me both. I'll be at the boarding house for a few days if you do remember anything.'

'I'll remember that part, Captain

Jody. Do you want this letter back?'

'No. I know it word for word.'

'This man Jesse Chayne. Who was he?' the girl asked with a sudden, penetrating look.

'My brother. If it makes any difference,' he added disappointedly. 'Sorry to have troubled you.'

★　★　★

From the cover of a streetside cottonwood, Royston Poole saw the door open, Ben's high shape against the pale, hallway light. He unbuttoned his long coat, took it off and moving forward threw it across the pickets of the Kings' side fence. At the sight of Ben, a rush of angry blood took the edge off the gripping chill. He stood watching, held his breath, trying to make out something Willow King was saying. Then he hissed quietly as Ben left the porch and made his way towards the street.

Poole had picked his spot carefully. He let Ben get within three or four strides before he stepped from the inky shadows.

'Hold up there, feller,' he challenged.

Ben drew up short as he made out Poole's shape against the background of bright snow. He looked the man over warily, his senses quickly tuning for trouble.

'Hell, if you've been waiting for me, you must be half-froze,' he offered. 'What went on back there was nothing personal, friend. Just nothing to do with you.'

'No one pushes me around. No one, you hear?'

If the man was carrying a gun, Ben decided he didn't intend to use it. 'No one pushed you around . . . except the girl, maybe,' he chaffed, his tone almost affable. 'So, whatever it is you've got in mind, forget it.' Ben cursed under his breath at the thought of a messy fist fight in the snow. Dipping his head, he started on his way, even stepped aside to go around the man.

That was when Poole lunged. He

struck out savagely and unexpectedly, but Ben's senses had been ground sharp. He snapped his head back and Poole's fist just grazed the underside of his jaw. It took the breath out of him though, set him up well for the hard right that followed to his chest. For a second he stood paralyzed by the pain across his ribs, watched Poole take a backward step, set his shoulders for another swing.

But the man slipped on a footfall of hard-packed snow and Ben had his chance. In a short, fast movement, he whipped the heel of his right hand up, then down, caught Poole in the flesh above his collarbone. He spread his boots for purchase, and accompanied by a fervent curse, threw a second pulverizing blow. The man was still off-balance, but with all the weight of his body, Ben had hit him full in the middle of his face. Now, Poole crumpled, fell slowly to the snowy sidewalk. Half-smothered, he took one, big grunting breath against the stillness.

Ben threw a quick, anxious glance at the King house, but it had returned to darkness and the door was closed. He bent down, and dragging at Poole's clothing managed to pull and roll him onto his back. Then he jerked his coat open and drew a short-barrelled .36 from its holster under the man's left arm. He thought for a second, then threw it out to the deep snow across the street.

'Somebody told me I was supposed to be standing you and your crew whiskey sweeteners,' he mused. Then he turned and walked back towards the main part of town.

4

Ben's temper took a few moments to settle, but his thoughts didn't. The confrontation with a Twin Rivers co-worker made as much sense to him as coming four hundred miles to ask questions of a dead man. He thought he was living with the ill-fortune that had dogged him since Brigadier Bonnie refused to grant him leave for a reckless, personal mission. The only help he'd had recently, was less than ten minutes ago when Royston Poole lost his footing and slipped in the snow. Still, it more or less confirmed what Ralph Curtin had said, the man was a mean son-of-a-bitch.

He asked himself what came next and found that he didn't have much of an idea. As far as any understanding of Jesse's death was concerned, he was precisely where he'd been nearly five days ago. Doctor King might have known what he was looking for, but if he had, the upshot got buried with him.

Walking at a pace, and deep in thought, Ben was in the middle of town before noticing that the main street was now fairly deserted. He'd walked past the Black Robe Saloon before the discordant notes of a pianola and the thought of whiskey turned him about.

The saloon was crowded and noisy, pervaded with the eye-watering cut of stale booze, smoke and sweat. He made his way to the bar, within a couple of minutes was settling himself with the heat of strong liquor. But the ache in his chest from the punch he'd taken, was making him wonder if he'd made a mistake. Had he made an enemy of Poole, maybe ruined his chances of working for Ambrose Quill for two hundred dollars a month?

He stayed at the bar a further ten minutes, a second glass failing to lift him entirely from his concern. But then he got to thinking of how good a bed was going to feel after days and sleepless nights on stages and trains.

When he stepped out onto the boardwalk, the snow was falling again. It was coming down straight and soundlessly as he levelled with a narrow passageway a couple of buildings up from the saloon.

'Hey Jody,' a voice spoke harshly from the deep shadows.

'Hell, not again. Maybe it's some sort of trial,' Ben rasped under his breath. He stopped and turned to face the alleyway, saw the vague shapes of two men already moving out towards him. One held a carbine, the other one who circled behind him wore a blanket coat, and Ben recognized him. His name was Otto Miles — the heavy who'd helped himself to the seat on the train from Duckwater. And Ben knew that whatever happened next was more than a chance, ill-fated robbery.

'He's carryin' a hog leg,' the one with the carbine said.

Miles closed in on Ben and lifted his

jacket flap aside. 'Don't you go mindin' me,' he said quietly, as he jerked the .44 Colt from its holster. Then the other one stepped in and thrust his carbine's barrel hard into Ben's chest.

'Just step back off the street, an' be real careful,' he commanded flatly.

Ben looked down at the carbine, where it hurt, saw the man's thumb curled over the hammer.

'Back where?' he said, trying to create a lull. *If anyone else in this goddamn town lays a hand on me, I'll bust them apart*, was his actual thinking.

'Just move,' Miles answered him, moving up close again.

Ben realized it was part of the man's strategy to get up real tight, to help the intimidation. 'Suppose I stay right here?' he asked, attempting not to fall for it.

But Miles laughed. 'Hah, you hear what the gent says, Bast?' he said.

He was still carrying a harsh grin as the back of Ben's right forearm connected with Bast's carbine. The man couldn't even beat the upswing, and before his thumb could move, Ben had wrenched it from his grasp, slammed the butt sideways into Miles's hip.

'Army combat training,' he grated, 'comes in handy when you don't want to surrender.' With that, Ben then chopped the carbine's barrel hard across Miles's wrist, shoved him around the wall-corner of the alleyway. The man's head fell back against the clapboards and in the instant of blinding pain before consciousness briefly left him, he dropped Ben's Colt.

Ignoring the collapse of Miles, Ben turned as Bast was making a lunge for him. The man was making a grab for his holstered Colt with his right hand, and Ben took his outstretched left. He clutched at the man's sleeve, snatched him forward and down. Bast's head met the edge of the boardwalk with a dull thud and Ben lashed out with his boot. 'You scuttle around with alley rats and you get smashed like one,' he seethed.

In the shadowy darkness around him,

Ben could see very little. He sensed more than heard that Miles was up and coming for him, turned in time to see that now the burly man had his own Colt in his fist.

With Miles suddenly silhouetted against the snowy street, Ben sensed an advantage. He could have hurt the man real bad at that point, even killed him. All he had to do was step to one side, let Miles come for him and crack his skull. Instead, he dropped the carbine, steadied himself and swung a tight-balled right fist, hard at the centre of Miles's forehead.

He heard the man's Colt bang against the boards of the building wall, but his body came on. Ben hit him with a short chop to the back of the head, stepped away as the man fell silently into the snow.

He was winded, sobbing for breath, and he leaned against the corner of the building, dragging in deep lungsful of air. He looked along the street, saw no one in sight, either way. When someone came out of the Black Robe, a brief narrow wedge of yellow lamplight shone out across the snow, but whoever it was staggered a full turn, then lurched back into the saloon. He picked up his hat, lifted his Colt from the trampled snow, and when he looked back, Miles was on his hands and knees.

He cursed, took a couple of steps forward to grab the man's big, loose-fitting coat and hauled him to standing. Then he slapped him sharply across his dark jowls.

'Listen, seat-snatcher,' he snarled as Miles's head sagged. 'Go and tell Poole you weren't good enough. Tell him to send the sewing bee, next time.'

5

Six heavily-armed Yellowstone men lifted their boots through the drifted snow, scrambled aboard a railcar loaded with bridge timbers. In the pre-dawn dark, they started out from their tent camp, cursed and shivered all the way to the sidings at Chisel Canyon. When the train squealed to a halt, they piled off and headed for a blazing fire that was being fed by discarded ties. Meantime, the work crew and the freight wagons moved in on the flatcar. Within half an hour the wagons were fully loaded, their mule teams straining up the grade that had been dynamited from the rock face along the river. The day was already bright, although the sun hadn't risen much above the distant Bad Lands.

Harpers Gap was still mostly asleep as the sounds of the train passed through. But rousing himself at dawn had become too strong a habit for Ben to break. Standing at the window of his room, he yawned, stretched tentatively and watched a line of ox teams getting hitched to their freight at the far end of town. He was stiff and sore, and flexing his muscles made him wince at the pain across his ribs. His chin was tender from where Royston Poole's fist had grazed him, and his knuckles hurt. But he'd worked something out during a fitful night's sleep and was still secure in his resolve to carry on with his task.

He shaved, took a clean flannel shirt from his grip. Dragging it around his aching shoulders he went back to the window, looked out over the town again. For a few minutes he watched distractedly as the first, strong sunlight touched snow-blanketed roofs. He guessed that the snow would be gone from this lower country before the day was out.

The town, he saw, was built across one of many upper benches that pocketed the mountains. He could make out a deep notch that cut north-west through the pine-dotted foothills, estimated it was the mouth of Chisel Canyon. Backing the lower tier of hills, the white-hooded peaks of Crazy Bull Mountains thrust up towards a high layer of cottony cloud. But directly west, clear blue sky roofed the pass through which the Musselshell roared down from the high country. It was the fight for that pass that was bringing all this activity to Harpers Gap.

Next, the thought of food turned him from the window. He was buckling on his gunbelt when sounds from the hallway, made him stop and listen cautiously for a moment. Then he shrugged, pulled on his jacket and picked up his hat. But as he reached to open his door, someone knocked. It was the inquisitive old clerk he'd spoken to last night in the lobby.

'You got a visitor,' he baldly announced. 'She's waitin' for you in the sittin' room. It's at the far end o' the hall.'

'Yes, I saw it, thanks. Did she say who she was?' Ben asked, thinking of Willow King, but knowing it wasn't.

'No. But she ain't been in town long. Sure is a looker, slim as a bedslat too,' the man said, already turning away as he spoke.

The excitement Ben had felt a moment ago at his imagining was instantly replaced by something more circumspect. He wheeled from his room and, with a cautious smile, walked to the end of the hall. He paused at the open door, waited for his visitor to turn and see him.

'Ben,' she cried elatedly, rising from one of three plush chairs.

'I should have known you'd surprise me,' he replied, his smile suddenly gone as he stepped forward into the room. 'But I still am, Eady.'

'Foolish man. Did you think I'd stay away?' Edith Bonnie put her head to his shoulder. 'You are pleased to see me, aren't you Ben?' she murmured. 'After all, we share a *betrothal*.'

'No, no it's not that, Eady,' Ben started with a shake of his head. 'It's just that in places like this, you learn to control that sort of feeling,' he said, her openness momentarily confusing him.

With a more serious face, Eady took a step back. 'You're thinner, Ben. And you look worried. What's going on?'

'Well, I've not had breakfast yet,' he suggested wryly. 'And probably worried because I'm going to be too late for any.'

Eady's expression now held a touch of concern. 'So, you're *surprised* I came? That's not quite the same as *glad*, is it?'

'I'm glad enough, Eady. I just hadn't expected you.'

'No, you had something else on your mind.' Ben didn't respond, and Eady backed off again, clasped her fingers around the top of the chair. 'You've got to give this up, Ben,' she continued after another silent moment. 'Pa told me you were very defiant . . . stubborn . . . that close to being insubordinate. He said, you've worked around mules for so long, you've started to act like one.'

Ben raised a slow smile, but it told Eady very little, so she went on. 'So far you've done nothing we can't mend. Pa's letter said he was holding your resignation. If you go back now, he can smooth things over — everything can be forgotten.'

'Well, that's good to know, Eady, but it won't be quite *everything*,' Ben returned.

A flick of anger showed in Eady's grey eyes, and she turned her head away, impatiently. 'Suppose someone did kill Jesse. Wasn't he always in trouble, Ben?' she said. 'An' wasn't it always over some woman or other?' Eady made *woman* sound like a term for something improper.

'He was my brother,' Ben snapped back. 'Unlike you, Eady, I didn't have much more family than him. Sure he was touched by the wildness stick, but he'd never back-shoot anyone. That was for someone else.'

'And you're going to find out who it was?'

'Yes, that's exactly what I'm goin' to

do . . . why I came all this way.'

Eady's shoulders drooped as she appeared to become resigned. 'Well in that case, I'll stay here. We'll get the circuit sin-buster to marry us. They can do that can't they?'

Ben had the sudden thought that that was Eady's way of getting him to stop going after his brother's killer, its associated risks. He gave her a glance that meant no discussion. 'Yes, your pa would really like that,' he answered her back. 'No, Eady, we'll wait until I've done what I set out to do.'

'Yes, there's a change in you, Ben,' she said. Then she stepped away from the chair and moved slowly back towards him, let the closeness work. Much of the pique seemed to leave her and she looked around the room with a small resigned smile. 'I guess I can put up with this for a day or two. But right now I'm so tired. It wasn't a journey, for sleeping on.'

'I was beginnin' to wonder how you'd got here,' Ben said. 'Last night they said the stage couldn't make it.'

'They told *me* that,' Eady replied. 'I paid a teamster twenty dollars to drive me across.'

Ben smiled meagrely, thought about suggesting she should have waited for the next work train.

'How dirty are the beds?' she asked.

'They're not,' he said slowly. 'Bugs don't take to the cold. But this town really isn't your style, Eady.'

'Maybe not, but it's where I can keep an eye on you, Ben Jody.'

Ben recalled Quill's comment about Noel Bonnie being a tolerant man, reckoned it wasn't quite the word he would have chosen to describe the daughter.

'I'll go see about rooms . . . your luggage. Perhaps we can have some breakfast?' he suggested.

'No thanks, Ben. I don't think my stomach can take anything at the moment. If you ask the clerk to come here, that'll be fine. Come and see me later this afternoon.'

Ben knew this was Eady's way of telling him he was inconveniencing her. He'd changed all right, wasn't quite the man she'd known back at the post. 'I'll see if they'll let you have this and the adjoining room,' he said. His tone was obliging, but there was little doubt it held her at arm's length.

'No, please. Just tell the clerk I'd like to see him,' she reciprocated.

'OK,' he said with a compliant smile and went out into the hall.

Once out on the narrow, boarded walk, Ben started to feel uneasy over his reunion with Eady. He would usually give in to her slightest whim, an amusing sort of gallantry. But now their relationship was decidedly rocky, certainly prickly. He puffed against the cold, decided it wasn't something that couldn't be smoothed over, once back at the post. And best to get married with full dress. Officers of a certain rank were sticklers for formality.

It was when he'd reached a likely-looking eating house, ducking under its

47

hanging sign of a giant beefsteak, that he saw Otto Miles.

The man was leaning against the prop post of a false-front building, almost directly across the street. From a distance, Ben could see his swarthy face looked puffy and his lips swollen, the livid line of a deep cut running across one cheekbone. Huddled in his heavy, wool capote, he stood idly watching the townsfolk walk to and fro.

Ben stopped, waited for Miles's glance to swing his way. Miles blinked slowly as he took in Ben's appearance, then he looked away, indolently pushed out from the post and strode on down the plank walk. When he'd gone a dozen or so paces, Ben went into Carlo's Chop House, mildly interested that the man hadn't moved off through worry.

6

For one reason or another, Royston Poole awoke a little later than Ben. He too looked out from his window across the town, but unlike Ben, his thoughts were more engaged. He made out the leafless cottonwoods just beyond the edge of town, the roof of the King house, a thin plume of smoke rising from one of its chimneys.

Twenty minutes later, Willow King opened a back door of the doctor's house.

'Roy. This is early,' she said, surprised. 'The roosters are hardly through crowing.'

'I've not slept much,' Poole began. 'I made a fool o' myself, last night. Butting into somethin' that wasn't my affair. I'm sorry, Willow. I came to apologize.'

'Well you certainly *look* like you butted into something,' Willow responded with an expressive look. 'Was it to do with

Captain Jody? Were you trying to keep him from seeing me?'

'Yeah, something like that.'

Willow raised a smile at Poole's apparent regret. 'You did what you thought best,' she said. 'Perhaps you'll come in for some breakfast?'

'Thanks, yes. I guess it'll be a tad healthier than swallowing someone's fist.'

'I'm sure. Griddlecakes and coffee, shouldn't take too long.'

Poole smiled hesitantly as he followed Willow into the house. He was thinking that she'd got some colour back since late yesterday and her eyes were more lively. He'd only known her a little, but in the last two weeks he'd got to know her better, realized there was something else above and beyond the real motive for his morning call. It probably involved the stranger, Captain Jody, and he'd have to find out.

'What happens now?' he began. 'Do you think you'll stay on here?'

Willow brought a steaming pot of

coffee from the kitchen stove. 'I haven't decided yet,' she said solemnly as she filled his cup.

'Didn't your pa have a family?'

'Yes, up in Williston . . . near where the rivers meet. But I can't just up and leave until another doctor comes. Do you think I should go?'

'Well, it's a big house.'

'I can look after us both, if that's what you're suggesting, Roy,' she replied. 'Food's ready in a minute or two.'

Poole watched her go back to the stove, decided to come straight out with what was playing on his mind. 'You ever thought of marrying?' he asked.

Willow turned around, threw him a searching look. 'Not much point without an opportunity,' she answered. 'Of the only two eligible men I've seen in recent months, one had scabies, the other one had an arm hanging off. Some of the others were probably too sick to notice me.'

'I haven't got any limbs hanging off, Willow, and I'm not too sick to notice.'

She gave a quick surprised smile, but it soon changed to mischievousness. 'I guess it's too early for you to have looked in the mirror this morning?'

Poole took a moment, struggling to hide the irritation of Willow's remark. 'Yeah, I know,' he said, 'I'd better own up. Me and your visitor had a bit of a scuffle. I got a smack in the mouth for it.'

'You had a fist fight with Captain Jody?' She was incredulous. 'Why?'

Poole picked up his cup and took a careful sip of the hot coffee. 'Because I'm jug-headed. And he did sort of push his way in.'

'He didn't, Roy, and you know it. But he did have good reason, as it turned out. You should have caught on when he said he wasn't going to leave.'

Poole waited for more, but Willow turned back to the stove. They'd been talking around the edges of the thing he'd come to get an answer to, so when he spoke again, he tried to sound more laid-back.

'I'd already told him about your father, so it wasn't some physic he'd come for,' he suggested.

'No, you're right about that,' was all Willow had to say.

As Poole sat trying to think up another way of getting an explanation, she brought him a plate of hot griddlecakes.

'Pa liked them three at a time,' she said, showing no sign of continuing the previous exchange.

There wasn't another opportunity for Poole to bring up the subject of Captain Jody, discreetly or otherwise. So, a half hour later when he left the house, his disgruntled mood was peppered with some concern. Willow hadn't only succeeded in side-stepping his clear proposal of matrimony, she'd ignored him querying the business between a goddamn pill roller and a goddamn Army officer.

*　*　*

Across the other side of town, Otto Miles was waiting impatiently outside the office of Poole's lumber-yard. He cursed when he saw the man coming, and walked up the street to meet him. He caught the angry set of Poole's face, wondered if it was the reminder of last night that still gripped him.

'I've found your soldier boy. He's at the Chop House havin' breakfast,' he said. 'You must've walked right past him.'

'Is he there alone?' Poole asked.

Miles nodded. 'Yeah, if you don't include sittin' down with half a steer.'

'I'll go and see him . . . have a talk.'

'He don't strike me as someone who backs off. You want me along?'

'No, we've already tried that. Wait for me at the yard,' Poole directed his man.

Poole found Ben sitting at the rear of the small eating house. Ben hardly raised his eyes as he pushed his chair a foot away from the table.

'Easy, Captain, I came to talk.' Poole said, taking a nearby facing seat. His

54

manner was calm, almost affable.

Now, Ben looked directly at him. 'I get indigestion real easy, mister, and you could have talked last night. What's changed?'

'Me, I guess,' Poole said, with an awkward grin. 'I was carrying a lot of steam last night. You told me to forget it, and I should have done.'

Without reply, Ben pushed the remains of his meat and gravy platter to one side.

'I was about to ask for her hand,' Poole continued. 'A man can get himself mighty muddled at such times.'

'Is that it?' Ben said, giving Poole more interest. 'You found me to talk about plighting your goddamn troth?'

'Hell, no. I was explaining my frame o' mind,' Poole replied. 'I was there assisting Willow with her affairs, or trying to. Perhaps I should have said so.'

'Perhaps. It wouldn't have made any difference,' Ben advised.

'So, what was it you came to see her about?'

'That's my affair. You could try asking her.'

'I already have.'

'There you go.' Ben realized then, that for some reason he was only whetting Poole's curiosity. And the one thing he still didn't want, was for Poole or anyone else to get too curious about him.

'So you've already been calling and she hasn't told you?' Ben waited for Poole to shake his head. 'It's like I said, our business, not yours,' he repeated. 'But as you're so troubled by it, I'll tell you. The truth is, there was some business between me and Cyrus King, and I didn't want to be last in line. Not very gracious of me, I know, and now I've spoken to his daughter, there's no business, anyway. So that's it feller. End of story,' he lied.

Now, Poole was more satisfied that it was a business matter that lay behind Ben's visit last night, told him that Captain Ben Jody might be someone he could use. Anyone who was ruthless enough to disregard a daughter's grief for her father, possessed valuable qualities.

'So what are you going to do now?' he asked.

'Depends. I'm on indefinite army furlough,' Ben said. 'I told you, there's one or two ideas on the stove. I might look to a short-term investment,' he continued with his exaggerations. 'I'm told that up in this territory, that's the best sort.'

Poole immediately ticked Ben off as a yellow leg deserter, someone who'd gone AWOL at the least, maybe even run off with military funds. 'Yeah, you were told right,' he said. 'Someone could double their dollars, if they knew where to put 'em. Why not let me show you?'

'I'll need a bit more than that. Give me an idea of what and where,' Ben said.

'Ties and bridge timbers . . . general railroad construction. Luckily, I've got the lumber yard. We could take a look now, if you've finished your breakfast.'

'And if I haven't, where do I find you?'

Poole nodded towards the north end of town. 'Hundred yards or so. You can't miss it. Incidentally, where'd you learn to brawl?' he added. 'I would have thought officers fought with fancy sabres and etiquette, not their fists.'

Ben smiled. 'Your mistake. You shouldn't believe everything you read in dime novels.'

'Hmm, funny,' Poole sided. 'And you owe me a nice .36 hideout. I was wearing it when we met.'

'It's in the snow near the King house. Send one of your hounds to sniff it out.'

'Yeah, well maybe I'll go myself. Don't leave it too long before stopping by.'

As Poole made his way back out to the boardwalk, he looked around for someone to bring him a cup of coffee. His feelings weren't as easy-going as the set of his features implied. With a white lie, he'd satisfied Poole's curiosity, maybe started to earn his wages for Ambrose Quill and the Twin Rivers Railroad Company. And if he could get on board with Poole, it should be a fairly simple matter to get the information Ralph Curtin wanted. Meantime, he'd get on with what had brought him to Harpers Gap in the first place, the uncovering of Jesse's killer.

Ten minutes later, he paid for his meal and stepped out onto the street. The strong, early sunlight was already taking the chill from the air, and he felt restless to get on. He stood for a minute or so wondering how to approach Harry Gedding, then something he'd said to Poole, gave him the start of an idea. He'd handle the matter as an investor might, make a bid for Jesse's half of their Silver Track freight business. There'd be no need to disclose his brother's real identity at this stage. He'd been living and working here as Jesse Chayne, so the name Jody should mean nothing to Gedding.

7

Since the day they'd pulled Jesse's body from the river, Harry Gedding had systematically logged the size and shape of his and Jesse's business. He had prided himself on knowing the income and expenditure sums at any hour of the day or night. As for the other holdings, some days he was too busy to make more than one or two entries in the Silver Track ledger. But today with the noon meal an hour gone, he was nearing a full stocktake. His foreman, Billy Dan, was due back with the wagon-load of supplies he'd driven to Harpers Gap for. But until he pulled in to the company yard, there was little more to keep Gedding busy.

He was estimating the tonnage of the baled hay in the loft, looking up when he saw the rider coming down the trail from Swimfish Cut. He thought at first the man was headed for Sam Paynter's camp, where men came and went from the guard tents at all hours of day and night. It was both a shortcut from the Windhammer road to the Yellowstone grade in the Canyon, and a normal stopover for any Twin Rivers man riding to Dirt Creek and beyond. He continued with his work, only glanced around when he realized the horse had turned in through the gate.

Ben rode his hire mount into the freight yard until he was a dozen feet from where Gidding was standing with his ledger.

'Afternoon. I'm looking for Harry Gedding,' he said, letting the reins drop. There didn't appear to be anyone else moving around the yard, but according to a description once contained in a letter from Jesse, he knew from the man's beard and short stature he'd just found him.

Gedding nodded. 'That's me,' he replied. But he knew the sometime cost of information, and didn't offer anything else.

'My name's Ben Jody. I heard in Harpers Gap you're looking for a new partner. With a two-man outfit, it must be a real blow,' Ben said.

'Yeah, it is, an' he was a good man.' Gedding looked at Ben trying to guess his intent, unsurprisingly thought he must be one of Royston Poole's men. Over the past few weeks Poole had made several offers for Silver Track. But neither him nor Jesse had any time for the man, and not for one moment had they considered selling their company to him. As the thoughts turned in his head, so did Gedding's unfounded gut feeling about Ben. 'Well you've had yourself a long cold ride out here for nothin' feller, 'cause nothin's for sale. Not now or in the foreseeable future,' he said.

'I was talking about Chayne's interest, not the whole kit an' caboodle,' Ben replied.

'Still a long cold ride. First off, there's his kin to consider, an' I ain't heard from anyone yet. Besides, I might decide to buy in myself.'

Ben worked up a thwarted grin. 'Huh, just my luck eh? One deal closes in front of you as another gets clinched behind.'

'If it's deals you're after, there's any number of 'em to be had in Swimfish,' Gedding said, indifferently.

'Yes, so I heard. Problem is, I want something within the law. Like most old cavalry, all I know about's horse dealing.'

Gedding shrugged, said nothing, so Ben went on. 'Supposin' there was a chance to buy Chayne's half o' the business. What price would you put on it?' he asked.

Gedding gave a slow shake of the head, pointed the ledger at a row of storage sheds. 'This is the first chance I've had to get a line on what's in stock. It'll take me a few days before I know what we're worth,' he replied.

For a few moments, Ben had a look around, took in the wagon sheds, workmen's cabin, smithy, cords of lodgepole. 'How about giving me an option on his share?' he suggested. 'I'd like to see the company work . . . wouldn't be aiming to lose money. I'd pay a fair price for a couple of month's option. Make it an open sale if an' when you do decide to sell. What do you say?'

Gedding was listening, but now he was looking out beyond the line of barns. From the direction of Swimfish's deep cut, he could see two riders headed towards his yard. For the shortest moment before he recognized Royston Poole and Otto Miles, he cursed under his breath, tried to hide a rising fear. Poole was raring to get his hands on the yard because freighting his own ties would just about give him a monopoly, allow him to demand any price of either railroad. Now, already convinced that Ben was a Poole man, Gedding thought they were resorting to more persuasive tactics. It wasn't a rumour that Poole had already forced more than one tie-camp competitor to sell up. In a near deserted yard with an armed stranger keeping him from summoning help, he cursed again, hoped to see Billy Dan driving down the road, that the crew cook or workshop smith would make an appearance.

He took a quick glance at Ben's Colt, convinced himself that the man was a hired gun and as such, more dangerous than either Poole or Miles. He did some quick thinking and, bearing in mind the situation, grunted out an acceptance of Ben's offer.

'Right now I could use a cash injection,' he said. 'Follow me before I change my mind.'

Gedding walked ahead to the hitch rail outside of the company office. 'We'll draw up an option,' he confirmed, waited a moment while Ben dismounted. Then he went into his office, stood behind his desk and drew its wide drawer open a few inches. He knew he'd feel a lot better switching the company ledger for his big Colt Dragoon. Deciding to play the deal the way it was being called, he took to his chair, picked up a pen and began writing. 'I'll make it simple,' he muttered more to himself than Ben. 'Jesse used to say that was one way o' puttin' truth in a pretty dress.'

'Sounds like a smart feller,' Ben returned with a wry smile. 'You could start by investing some of the money in a better-quality stove.'

Less than two minutes later, as Gedding was checking the gist of the basic option, Poole stepped into the office closely followed by Miles.

'Hello Gedding. Where's the rest of your crew?' Poole asked cordially before noticing Ben who was standing to one side of the door.

For a charged moment the two men eyed each other in surprised silence, and although he didn't understand, Gedding wasn't slow to notice.

'Captain Jody. We meet again,' Poole said in dead-pan tone.

Miles coolly stepped alongside Poole. But the look that crossed his face, made Gedding think maybe he'd been mistaken in taking Ben Jody for a Poole man.

'You two know each other?' he asked pointedly.

'Our paths have crossed,' Ben said and smiled tightly.

Poole now sensed Miles's agitation. 'Ease off, Otto,' he warned, half turning to his man. Then he took a deep breath, made a visible effort to relax and looked back to Gedding. 'I was hopin' to talk somethin' over,' he said. 'You got a minute or two?'

'If that's all it takes, I'll listen,' Gedding answered.

Poole hesitated, made it obvious that he wasn't overjoyed at Ben Jody's presence. But he could tell things weren't going to change. 'I've got a haul that's bogged down. I'd like you to take it back.'

Gedding resolutely shook his head. 'Can't take the chance, an' you know why. I've lost most part of a good hickory wagon, along with two spare wheels, an' an axle. I'm also down four big mules an' I got a driver who's stove up for weeks. All that's from one goddamn accident, so I'm through with night hauls.'

'Hmm, I thought that's the way you'd see it. Suppose I supply you with a guard . . . one for every wagon?'

Again Gedding shook his head, this time with a weary grin. 'What the hell use is a guard when the goddamn road caves in,' he snorted. 'Besides, I got business enough not to take the chance.'

Poole changed his tack. 'So who'd have it in for you bad enough to rig the accident?' he asked.

'Search me. Maybe they thought they'd be hurtin' you. It would sure put the brake on you gettin' your ties out. You've climbed the ladder fast, Poole. Maybe too fast.'

Poole nodded thoughtfully, let out a spare smile. 'Then that's made you a few friends, and you're putting me in a spot. I'm going to ask you again, Gedding. If I went to ten thousand, would you reconsider selling?'

'You go to wherever you like, Poole. To my simple mind, no sale actually means *no sale*. Money don't much come into it.' Gedding then nodded towards Ben. 'What's more, I wouldn't have all the say. The cavalryman here holds an option to buy Jesse's half o' the business if it comes up for sale.'

The bright gleam of anger at once flared in Poole's eyes. He stared unbelievingly at Ben.

'Since when? How come?' he rasped irritably.

Ben shrugged. 'I told you there was a few irons in the fire, or something to the effect. I was looking for a short-term investment, and just found it.'

Poole's glance swivelled back to Gedding. 'Let's hear it from you,' he said.

'You wanted it *all*, Poole. Jody wanted half.'

The look Poole then gave Gedding was openly hostile. 'We'll talk again on this,' he said, his voice almost a hiss. Turning without another word, he nodded to Miles and walked irately from the office. With a snatch that hurt the horse's mouth, Poole unknotted his reins, swung into the saddle and started back across the yard.

When Miles caught up with him, Poole was still seething with anger. They were turning the fence at the corner of the yard, headed towards the foot of the Swimfish trail when Miles spoke up.

'You lettin' him get away with that?' he asked.

'He already has,' Poole responded furiously.

Miles lifted his heavy sloping shoulders. 'This Captain Jody's become a real pest. If he's anythin' like Chayne, he'll sink his pincers in.'

'Yeah, we've met his sort before,' Poole agreed quietly. Then he held up his hand and reined in. Against the base of the perimeter fence, a pile of rotten bed planks from a garbage truck had caught his eye. He leaned over the fence, reached down and thumbnailed a sliver of the grease-smeared wood. 'Sometimes we get burned afore we learn,' he muttered.

Miles sat quietly, watched with puzzlement as Poole reached inside his coat, then gulped with understanding when the man flicked a match alight and touched it to the timber.

Within moments, the oily-saturated wood was throwing up a slim ribbon of bright flame. Poole kneed his mount closer into the fence where it ran tight against a rear wall of the Silver Track barns. For better leverage he stood high in the stirrups, managed to shove and collapse the planks against the base of the building's clinkered wall. Then, without a word, as if nothing had happened, he turned away and continued to ride towards the foot of the trail.

'Christ, I didn't mean you to do that,' Miles burst out as he rode anxiously alongside. 'If that lot catches, it'll go wildfire through them buildin's.'

'Yeah, that's what I was thinking,' Poole rasped. 'But Harry Gedding's accident prone, an' that's a fact.' Then the man levelled a frosty eye at Miles. 'You're not going soft are you?' he demanded.

'No. An' I ain't goin' lame in the brain, either. An' if *they* ain't, they'll know it was you an' me fire-raisin'.'

The two men stopped a quarter-mile above where the trail turned away from the lower canyon. At first there was nothing to see, then very faintly they saw a thin collar of smoke rising lazily into the cold, still air.

8

With no particular need for him to be back at the yard early, Billy Dan had taken his time on the drive from town. He was driving a mud wagon, loaded with goods that had been accumulating in the Harpers Gap freight warehouse for the past two weeks. Stacked around the general marketing, there was four sets of harness, some bolts and nails for the blacksmith, several tarpaulins, four barrels of flour and two blocks of salt.

Since there was no place for the mules to go except along the road that snaked down the canyon with the new grade, Billy had been daydreaming. He was leaning back against the seat, one foot on the brake, the other on a heap of county broadsheets that every now and again, he'd look at a picture, read a column from. From time to time, he'd reach over to the reins wound about the seat brace, give them a jerk and curse the team from an idle walk into a short-lived trot.

When the canyon widened and the yard came into sight, still nearly a mile below, Billy sat up and took the reins in hand. He didn't mind if Harry Gedding knew he'd been taking his time, but as foreman he made it a point to set a business-like example for the crew. And that was something Jesse Chayne had insisted on. 'Good man Jesse Chayne,' he asserted as his glance ran over the yard. 'Ain't goin' to be the same without him.'

He saw the wrecked freight wagon standing alongside the blacksmith's shop, and their stable boy, Amos, who was wheeling a muck barrow from the stables. Then he saw two riders near the foot of the Swimfish trail. He was curious when they stopped at the rear of the barns, so he reined in the mules, sat watching until they rode on. Ten minutes later, he was tapping his boot on the toe board, humming to himself, when he saw the smoke against the clear sky. It was a smudgy haze rising from the barn's roof, and he quickly realized what was happening. He cursed, leant forward with the ends of the reins and slashed the team across their hindquarters.

The mules went into their ungainly run so fast, it jolted him back onto the seat. He shouted himself into a throaty croak over the clamour of the pitching wagon, realized he was too far from the yard to be heard by anyone. He groped behind the seat for his carbine, managed to fire off three shots before the team panicked. He dropped the rifle, used both hands to control the frightened animals and keep the wagon on the road. When he recognized Harry Gedding, and a tall man he didn't, leave the office and look up toward him, he stood up again and waved, pointed towards the barn, yelling, 'Fire,' until his throat seized up. He saw Gedding head for the barn at a run, the other man drag off a fur coat and follow. Nathaniel Cobb emerged from his smithy, and, carrying a woodsman's axe, loped off across the yard.

The smoke from the barn's roof was coiling upwards now, thicker and dirtier grey. Billy cursed, dragged the team off the road and down across the cedar-dotted slope. He was a hundred yards out from the barn, could more clearly see the man who was pitching blazing bales from the loft. When one of the wheels suddenly sunk into softer ground, the front axle slewed and he jumped from the seat, ran for the rest of the way.

'Billy. That's Ben Jody. He's tryin' to make a break,' Gedding shouted pointing up to Ben. 'Get up there an' help him. If we don't stop it spreadin', they'll all go up.'

Billy could see that from under the peak of the barn's roof, flames were now starting to lick through the smoke. He climbed the fence, dropped inside and ran for the ladder that led up to the loft. Above him he heard the sound of smashing timber, looked up to see the man named Jody pull himself through an opening in the roof. For a moment he watched as Ben scrambled up to the roof peak, began hammering through the shingles.

Cobb ran up to Billy and handed him his axe. 'Get this to him,' he shouted. 'You use your bare hands if you have to. I'll go get a team an' a drag chain.'

Billy took the axe and climbed the ladder as fast as he could. He could see how they might save the run of barns by collapsing its burning end, create a break from the other buildings. At the top of the ladder he could hear the pounding of Ben's hammer and he started in under the roof. He worked his way over the hot smouldering bales, but was soon out of breath, started to cough at the acrid bite of trapped, billowing smoke. He decided to go forward, climb back out where Ben Jody was, make his way to safety along the roof to the far end of the barns. He'd clear a space by chopping away

77

the partitions, let the fire burn itself out behind him. But the hole in the roof had created a through-draft, and bales from all sides started to burst into flames. A red curtain barred his way forward and tossing the axe up ahead of him, he pulled himself onto the highest bale. He gagged for breath, but a painful cough gripped his chest. Now, he couldn't see the hole in the roof. All he could hear was the hiss and crackle of burning, and panic seized him. He laid flat on his stomach, rolled from the smother of heat and smoke as weariness overcame him. He tried to drag himself back to the edge of the stacked bales, but couldn't find the strength.

Through the noise and bright spread of flame, he heard the clink of chains, the distressed whinny of a frightened mule. 'Hey Cobb, where the hell are you?' he rasped in vain. Then the hot, deep darkness came and he tried again. 'Where the hell's anyone?'

★   ★   ★

When his sledge-hammer finally broke through the shingles close above the eaves, Ben turned and climbed wearily back up the slope of the roof. 'Why don't you send up some help?' he shouted. But, due to the clouding smoke, he couldn't see much around him or below, and his plea was as much to himself as anyone else. His shoulders and arms ached, his hands were raw with blisters and, coughing uncontrollably, he was desperate for a lungful of fresh air. As he gained the ridge he blinked against the smoke, stared towards the yard below where Harry Gedding and Amos were hauling on a length of iron chain. They had turned one end around a corner post of the blazing barn, and beyond them, Nathaniel Cobb was pinning the other end to the swingle-tree of a draw mule.

A sudden gust of smoke that rose up through the chewed shingles, warned him that time to save the barn and escape was fast running out. He lifted the big hammer, put all his weight behind it and smashed down in a great arc. The steel head crushed through the shingles and fractured the collar beam in a single stroke. Then he backed a half stride, cursed violently before swinging again.

When he got close to the eaves he paused and yelled, 'Drag the goddamn barn apart. Pull now.'

Through the fog of smoke he saw Gedding lift his hand, and Cobb who immediately slapped the mule across its rump, shouted for it to move.

'Where's Billy?' Gedding called out. But Ben didn't understand and shook his head, lifted the hammer again as the roof swayed beneath him. He stumbled back, but the shattered beam started to crack under his feet. Part of the roof swung away as it broke from its struts, and as a ball of flame rolled through the gap, he scuttled back up to the ridge.

'For God's sake hurry up,' he yelled again at the men below, cursed and kicked several flaming shingles down at them.

Cobb, dragged violently against the mule's traces, watched as the line of the chain pulled tight. Moments later, the blazing end of the barn swayed, leaned at a critical angle until the whole flaming mass began to topple. Bales started falling from the loft, thudded to the ground in a mass of exploding sparks and flying embers. Tongues of fire shot skyward, and with a cracking and groaning of burning timber, the end of the barn came crashing to the ground.

As Ben backed off towards escape at the other end of the barn, he shouted down through the firey mayhem. 'I saw someone down there. Get him out.'

Gedding realized who was missing and started running. 'It's Billy,' he yelled. 'He's in them goddamn bales.'

Amos, his young face now a mask of distress, caught up with Gedding. He stood beside him, frantically clawed at the smoking bales that had spilled from the end of the loft.

'Must be like a hay oven, Boss,' he cried out as a pillar of smoke swirled low along the yard fence, curled thickly around their legs. 'How can he be alive?'

'Dunno, but he is,' Gedding said, putting his shoulder to a hundred-weight bale. 'Let's get this off him.'

Nathaniel Cobb helped Gedding and Amos lift the bale. Cursing quietly at the sight of Billy's blackened face, the tatters of his shirt and blistered shoulders, the blacksmith lifted him in his massive arms, carried him around the barn and over to the bunkhouse.

'Thanks Nate. I'll do what I can for him,' Gedding said after Billy had been carefully laid on a bunk. 'You go put the roan to the buggy an' bring back Doc King.'

9

Willow King didn't take much to being reminded of her father's death or his burial. She was just about to close the door after removing a wreath of dried flowers, when Nathaniel Cobb came running down the front path.

'Ma'am, we need the doc real bad,' he called out anxiously. 'A man's been burnt out at Swimfish, an' we reckon there's some bones broke. Tell the doc I've got a buggy waitin'.'

Willow was bewildered for a moment, stood staring at the burly blacksmith. 'He died. It was just this week,' she said quietly. 'Haven't you heard?' She saw a stricken look cross Cobb's broad face and apologised. 'I'm sorry, that wasn't meant to be a question. Of course you haven't heard. I can attend for him, though,' she added on impulse.

'You ma'am?' he breathed, his look

becoming worried again. 'I hadn't thought o' that. We'll be usin' the Swimfish trail. It's hard goin', but there's no other way o' gettin' there in good time.'

'Well we're sure wasting good time, talking about it. Let's get going,' Willow said. 'I'll need ten minutes.'

'There ain't anyone else in ridin' distance,' Cobb said, half an hour later on the trail towards Swimfish. 'If it had been one o' the mules, I'd have done somethin' myself.'

'I'll take that as a compliment,' Willow replied with a lean smile. 'Are you sure we're going to make it? Your roan looks all in,' she said, noticing the animal's gleaming flanks.

'The trail's a tight fit in places, but passable since the snow-melt. We'll get there,' Cobb asserted.

Willow was going to say it was *staying* there that worried her, but didn't think it was the right time. She set her feet against the footboard and wrapped an arm around her pa's medical bag.

At the fence corner, beyond the gate of the Silver Track yard, Ben and Harry Gedding were peering anxiously up the Swimfish trail. Sweat-grimed, and with only strong coffee inside them, they stood exhausted and impatient. In the deepening gloom of first dark, Gedding took out his watch. 'Almost four goddamn hours. If that ain't Nate comin' down the cut, Billy's in real trouble,' he muttered.

'Yeah, poor kid,' Ben answered back.

In the yard beyond the still smouldering ruin of the big barn, Amos and one of the drivers were unloading the goods from Billy's mud wagon. Beside them, another driver was unhitching a high-bodied brake he'd brought in from Dirt Creek.

During the next few minutes, Ben quietly pondered on Gedding, his honesty and consideration. He wanted to be sure that nothing had come between him and Jesse, nothing that in any way, could have been responsible for Jesse's

85

death. Ben didn't really think there was any need to doubt the man, more that he, himself was blinkered in his judgment. This got him to thinking of Eady Bonnie and her father's accusation of mulishness, and suddenly he wanted to be back in Harpers Gap, sharing her company.

'It's them,' Gedding exclaimed, staring into the falling light. 'But there's a woman. Who the hell . . . ?'

A moment later, Ben realized who was sitting beside Nathaniel Cobb. 'Was it Doc King he went to get?' he asked Gedding.

'Yeah. He's the only sawbones this side o' Windhammer.'

'I didn't know that,' Ben said. 'You see, that's his daughter, Willow King. She'll have come because the doc's dead. She buried him yesterday.'

'Christ,' Gedding cursed, turning quickly to look at Ben. '*Yesterday?* How the hell did that happen?'

'I heard he got snake bit,' Ben said, his attention still with Willow.

'Hell,' Gedding muttered wearily. 'There's always somethin' waitin' to kill you.'

Cobb was within shouting distance now. 'I brought Miss Willow. The doc ain't — '

'I know,' Gedding interrupted. 'I just found out. We're thankful you could come, Miss King,' he added, stepping past Ben. 'I'm sorry about your pa. I sometimes think this is a place where danger don't walk on by.'

'Yes, thank you. I hope we've got here in time,' she said kindly, her glance moving to Ben. 'Good evening Captain.'

'You'd better come straight on in,' Gedding said, noting something pass between the two.

Ben moved forward, took the medical bag as Willow stepped down from the buggy. He indicated that she follow Gedding, as Cobb handed the reins of the roan over to Amos.

'So you're the stranger who single-handedly saved the yard?' she said with an inquisitive look.

'Not quite. I had some costly help,' Ben conceded, immediately got to wondering how he could have been that preoccupied last night not to notice her arresting looks, her tallness.

Willow nodded in consideration. 'I know,' she said. 'How are you progressing with your own affairs, Captain?'

'Some, I guess. But I'd hardly call it *progress*,' he answered, hoping she wasn't going to say something unthinking and give him away.

'Is this man I've come to see, very badly hurt?' she more fittingly continued, her expression almost intimate. 'In helping my pa, I've done little more than lance boils or bandage sprains.'

'And I'm used to seeing field casualties . . . some horrors you can hardly imagine,' he said, forcing his attention to what she was saying. 'So between us we should get him back on his feet. I reckon it's the burns that need tending. And he must have taken a bang on his head. He's been out of it for a few hours.'

'Is his breathin' irregular . . . noisy?'

'Steady, I guess. Like he's sleeping.'

'Well, let's hope he is.'

'Cobb's goin' to clear the boys out,' Gedding said as they approached the bunkhouse. 'You'll have the place to yourself tonight, miss.'

'Thank you,' Willow replied. 'I won't be going anywhere until I've done all I can.'

'Yeah I know. We'll get you back home as soon as possible,' Gedding offered.

Ben smiled more easily, said he'd call in later. Then he backed off, stood quietly beyond the fall of the lamplight as Willow pulled up a chair alongside Billy.

Until this afternoon, he'd been certain of his loyalty and purpose. Eady Bonnie for one, hunting down Jesse's killer for the other. Yet his affecting interest was no longer on Eady and, like he'd told Willow, he'd just taken risks that hadn't remotely helped him unravel the mystery of Jesse's death. So he was a tad confused, strongly tempted to put right the half truths he'd told Harry Gedding. He reckoned he could get along with him, and even now, there appeared to be profitable opportunities for Silver Track.

For Ben, an alternative life would be a union with Eady and the insular world of an Army post. And for her, an existence anywhere near Harpers Gap wouldn't exactly amount to civic or social improvement. The inconsistent ideas were winding through his mind when someone shouted his name, brought him out of his reverie.

'Ben,' Gedding yelled as he strode towards him, issuing a stream of livid, staccato cursing. 'By God, I'll kill the bad-livered son-of-a-bitch. You hear me?' he exploded. 'Billy saw it all. Saw him messin' with somethin' near the old garbage truck. He's only just cottoned on to what he was up to.'

'What are you talking about? Who did Billy see?' Ben asked as Gedding ran breathlessly out of words.

'Royston Poole. He was settin' fire to

the old planks beside the barn.'

'Billy just told you that?'

'Yeah. He couldn't buy me, so he tried to burn me out. Jesse was right. It's Poole who's behind the fires that's hit the tie camps, an' busted up the crews. He just about owns every last camp there is out here.'

'But this isn't one of them,' Ben contended.

'No, it's more'n that. We freight most of his lumber to market, goddamnit. If he gets his hands on our Silver Track, he'll have a cartel . . . name his own price.'

'So why did he try and burn you out?'

'Because I already turned down his ten thousand. Goddamnit, you were there. With me out o' the way he'd bring in his own wagons. I think it's called, takin' out the middle man.'

'Well you should get even, not angry,' Ben said. 'I know he's got a lumber yard in Harpers Gap. But from what you say, there must be a tie camp

91

somewhere out here?'

'Yeah. It's upriver, 'twixt here an' Dirt Creek. What you thinkin'?'

'Does it carry much timber?'

'Sure. That's where all them ties come from,' Gedding said, allowing a mischievous smile to cross his face. 'You mean fight fire with fire?' he threw in as the idea dawned. 'Yeah, an' I'm just in the goddamn mood.'

'You'll need help,' Ben suggested.

Gedding was already turning away as he spoke. 'No I don't,' he said. 'This is somethin' I can handle on my own.'

Ben shrugged, started out after him towards the corral. 'Listen to me a moment. There's something I've got to tell you.'

'I'll be back in a couple of hours. Tell me then.'

'It might make a difference.'

'Not to what I'm goin' to do.'

'I'm Jesse's brother.'

Gedding stopped abruptly. 'An' how's that? Your name ain't Chayne. Or wasn't that *his* name?'

Ben shook his head. 'Jesse had his reasons for calling himself Chayne. Didn't he ever mention having a brother in the Army?' Ben asked.

'He might've done. But that ain't *such* a thing, is it?' Gedding said. 'Why didn't you tell me before you bought in?'

'Because I had to be sure of you.'

'Sure o' me in what way?'

'To tell you Jesse didn't drown.'

'Didn't drown? What are you sayin'?'

'There was no accident. Doc King wrote me. He didn't say in as many words, but it was what he was trying to tell me. He upped and died before I could get here, though.'

Gedding heaved a deep sigh. All of a sudden things were happening too fast, and he couldn't take it all in. It was a long moment before he spoke again. 'You ain't sayin' that the doc . . . ? You sure of all this?'

'About Jesse, yes. About the doc, not so much.'

Gedding shook his head as though to

clear his mind. 'Who the hell would've wanted to kill Jesse?'

'You'd know more about that than me, Harry. That's why I'm telling you before you go and cremate Royston Poole's tie camp.'

'It weren't *him*. Not Poole,' Gedding differed. 'Jesse only met him the once. It was the first time he tried to buy us out.'

'You said Jesse turned him down. Said he had no time for him.'

'That's right. It went for both of us. But you don't kill a man for *that*, do you?'

'It's been done for a lot less,' Ben said with little enthusiasm. 'I knew a drill sergeant once who had his dog shot to bits because he was plug ugly. The sergeant, that is. OK, so it wasn't Poole,' he went on. 'But he sure as hell burned down our barn.'

Gedding gave a slow smile. 'Maybe I will need your help,' he said.

10

It was seven o' clock in the evening when Royston Poole took a table in the dining room of the boarding house. The tables were quite full, yet Poole had one to himself. The waitress came quickly, exchanged a customary welcome before taking his order.

'Thank you Alice. I'll have it somewhere 'twixt rare and still kicking,' Poole confirmed as he usually did.

While Poole was waiting, he let his attention stray to a neighbouring table, where a slight and well-dressed girl was sitting. Not someone who's spent too many hours behind a ploughshare, he thought, then curiously wished he'd taken the time to change from the suit he'd spent half a day in the saddle in.

It was only a moment or two before Eady Bonnie became aware of Poole's regard. She seemingly ignored the attention, but she'd seen him come in, take the side table that was obviously a personal reservation. His stature and rugged looks made a fairly explicit impression, unlike her growing irritation with Ben Jody's tardiness.

She was already disenchanted at the shortcomings of Harpers Gap, so when the waitress brought Poole his meal before hers, she became even more irritated.

'Will I be sitting here waiting for much longer?' she asked coolly, as the girl walked past her table.

'I shouldn't think so, ma'am. But we are quite busy,' the girl replied.

'Yes, particularly with *that* table,' she said, with a nod in the direction of Poole. But, not wanting to make a fuss, she didn't raise her voice. 'I'm actually getting quite hungry,' she added.

A half hour later, Eady walked into the sitting room at the end of the hall. Sitting in one of the plush chairs by a street window, Poole was half-facing her.

'Ma'am,' he said, getting to his feet,

removing his Stetson in a showy expression of civility. 'My name's Royston Poole, and I'm at your service.'

Eady half-smiled. 'No doubt there's some that would be interested in seeing how that works out,' she said drily.

Poole thought for a short moment then nodded. 'Well, one way's if you're thinking of eating here again. I'm sure you're used to better-quality fare than's normally on offer. I could ensure some of it finds its way onto your plate.'

'Yes, I couldn't help noticing a certain influence with the service,' Eady said.

'Being a leading businessman has its perks.' Poole stepped to one side, as he spoke, motioned to his chair as he pulled another alongside it. 'Would you care to sit awhile and watch the street? It's no Alhambra, but there's precious little else to do at this time of day.'

'At *any* time of day, from what I've seen so far.' Eady laughed lightly and without sentiment, hesitated an appropriate moment before sitting down. 'For

a moment,' she answered. 'I'm expecting someone.'

'Of course,' he said sitting beside her.
'Possibly a mutual acquaintance?'

'Anything's possible, although he's
only just come to town. His name's Ben
Jody, Captain of Cavalry.'

Poole flinched unnoticeably, attempted
to hide his increased interest. 'Jody? I
guess it's a small coincidence for a town
this size, but yes, I do know him. I met
him only last night.'

Eady wasn't to know the heavy irony
behind Poole's smile as he continued.
'In fact it was a business matter.'

A look of alarm touched Eady's
eyes, and she responded a tad quickly.
'Whatever it is, I trust it's a matter that
won't keep him here in Harpers Gap.
Not for too long, anyway. My name's
Edith Bonnie, and Ben and I are to be
married, don't you know?' she added
lightly in an attempt to moderate her
anxiety.

Poole nodded amiably. 'Well, my
compliments to you both, Miss Bonnie.

If marriage was a business contract, I'd say Captain Jody got the best of the deal.'

Eady looked at Poole in a more thoughtful, considered way. 'Thank you. Perhaps there is a way you can help me,' she suggested.

'I've already made the offer. Just as long as it's lawful,' he added with a broader smile.

But now Eady tried to look uncomfortable and ill at ease. 'When I said I hoped it wasn't something to keep Ben here, it's because he shouldn't really be here at all,' she said quietly.

'He shouldn't?'

Eady decided to continue her tactic, although she wasn't sure now whether it was out of boredom or straightforward loneliness. Poole wasn't as crude as some folk she had encountered during the day, and the opportunity of a sympathetic listener was tempting. Besides, she actually did have concerns about Ben.

'No, he shouldn't. And I'm not the

only one who thinks so,' she replied firmly. 'Last week Ben resigned his commission. He threw away a fine career on nothing more than a wild notion.'

Poole frowned. 'There's not many men who haven't done something foolish along the way . . . something they regret. But there's usually a reason behind it, and I'm sure that goes for your good captain.'

'Yes, I appreciate that Mr Poole. But Ben's reason is a foolish revenge mission.'

'Revenge mission?' Poole queried. 'Here in Harpers Gap?'

'It's where his brother died. Ben's got it into his head there's something wrong.'

'What was his brother's name?' Poole asked. 'I might have been acquainted with him, too.' Now there was a discretion in Poole, but it would have taken a more attentive eye that Eady's to detect.

'Jesse. Did you know him?'

Once again Poole set his face to mask his actual and instant thinking. 'There's someone by the name of Jesse Chayne who runs a freighting business up Windhammer way . . . Swimfish.'

'That's him. Him that was. He was drowned, and Ben insists it wasn't an accident . . . says there's no such thing.'

'An' what do *you* think?'

Eady shook her head in frustration. 'Who's ever to know, other than the person who Ben's suspicious of. There's no evidence that I know of, yet he's thrown everything, and I mean *everything*, to the four corners by coming here. Right now, I'm not sure what to do or what to think. Do you, Mr Poole?'

Poole's mind was still running fast. 'Well I know nothing of their relationship, but maybe you could cut him some slack,' he offered with slight consideration. 'His brother would have been someone he'd known for some time,' he smiled sparingly. 'So he'd probably have come anyway.'

'Hmmm. But for how long? My father is his commanding officer, and he's shelving his resignation in the hope that Ben will come to his senses.'

'So, bearing all this in mind, you want him out of here, and back in the fold? Is that it?'

Eady nodded mutely, muttered some sort of regret for voicing her troubles.

Poole eased down in his chair as if in concerned thought. 'You know, army captains are resolute once their minds are made up. They have to be. And from what I know of him, I'd say he was that in spades, and a whole lot more. This means a great deal to you, doesn't it?' he added after a few moments of weighty silence.

'What do you think, Mr Poole?'

The man tilted his head in a slow nod. 'I think matchmaking's not my specialty, and I'd be working against my own interests. But you're a heck of a lot more decorative than all my usual clients.'

'I'm tempted to use whatever looks I

may have, Mr Poole. But that's against my better nature and there's absolutely no one else I can turn to.'

'We'd have to trick him in some way. An' that goes against my better nature Miss Bonnie,' Poole proposed.

'But you will help me?'

'Well, I'll try.' Poole nodded his assent. 'Sounds more interesting than toting lumber,' he said. His mind was almost exploding with thoughts about the true nature of Ben Jody and his assignment.

11

The poker game at Poole's tie camp usually started as soon as the supper dishes had been cleared away. It was two days after pay-day and Otto Miles was out to fill his pockets with the rest of the crew's hard earned wages.

At first, the man's cards ran poorly, and in the first hour he'd lost nearly twenty dollars. But gradually his luck changed, and he started to break even, began to win back a modest amount. He had just laid down a high club for a winning straight, was sweeping the money from the middle of the table when the camp cook yelled.

'Fire. The place is burnin'. Fire!'

The eyes of every man at the table swung towards the kitchen, then the door, then the window.

Miles caught the flickering rosy glow. Cursing, he hurled his chair clear and ran from the bunkhouse with the others close at heel.

The men jammed through the door. They spread out either side of Miles, stopped suddenly, stunned by what they saw ahead of them.

The sheer, climbing walls of the lower canyon were alight with a reflected glow. Plumes of flame leaped from the heap of ties and bridge timbers that lined the road on the river side. Beyond that, crew tents were ablaze, some of them already spewing smoke and blazing fragments of canvas into the inky black sky.

'Get movin',' Miles bellowed. 'Use anythin' to tip that stuff into the river. Go on,' he commanded, shoved the man standing nearest. Then he thought of something, cursed violently and turned towards the kitchen. 'Bring me that ol' cannon o' yours,' he yelled at the cook. 'Then get out there an' help *them*.'

Seconds later he broke open the big Colt's shotgun and checked its four chambers. 'I wonder what damage this'll do,' he said, grimacing at the ten gauge shot.

The belly strap was still loose when he vaulted onto the saddle of his mare. From back of the corral, someone shouted his name, but he paid no heed, kicked his spurs and took off at a dead run. He rode towards the deep shadows, down-river beyond the fires, on to where the lower canyon narrowed.

He dismounted, looped the reins around the saddle horn and slapped his horse to go further on down the road. He peered back towards the camp and the flickering shadows, then made for a low, gnarled juniper growing close to the roadside. He hunkered down, grounded the stock of the shotgun and listened for any sound. But all he could hear was the distant shouts of the crew, the whoosh and crackle of the fires.

He was guessing that whoever had set that blaze wouldn't have had time yet to circle the camp and strike this lower stretch of road. If he was right, the fire raiser would still be headed his way.

It was less than two minutes later that his hunch paid off. He saw the riders drifting toward him, recognized them both as they walked their horses close to the base of the canyon wall, out of the trees.

'They'll be on us soon. We've got to the road, let's move it,' he heard Harry Gedding say, lifting his horse to a trot.

He let Gedding go on past because it was the other man he wanted. As he rose up, moved from the shelter of the juniper, he cursed at his pains, the insult he'd taken from last night's fight with Ben Jody.

He let Ben walk his horse to within twenty feet of him, then he cocked the hammer of the big shotgun and stepped out into the road.

But Ben hadn't seen him yet. He was turned in the saddle, was taking a last look back at the roaring torches of the tents and timber. It was the horse that saw Miles. Only then did it come to a halt, and Ben looked around.

'This piece I'm carryin' will be a lot less heavy when it's fired,' Miles called out. 'An' my arms sure do ache. Don't go temptin' me, Captain Jody.'

Eying the gleam of the gun's long barrel, Ben cursed silently in recognition of the man who blocked the road ahead of him. When, after several seconds, Miles hadn't moved, Ben took a breath. 'If you're thinking of revenge, you've certainly got the advantage,' he suggested flatly.

But the man didn't respond and a long moment dragged on.

'Or have you froze because you're on your own and it's dark? Is that it?' Ben taunted daringly as the stress gripped him. 'Well feller, I'm no booger man, and you've got a mind to make up,' he muttered, wondering how far he had to go before Miles pulled the trigger. So he flicked the reins and, sensing the man's stare, he walked his horse steadily forward.

'I guess I'll just walk right on by,' he said, when he was only a few feet away.

'Shooting me in the back's about the only chance you'll ever get.'

He could feel his heart thumping wildly, the icy run of sweat between his shoulder blades. Then he wondered how far his mare had carried him beyond Miles, twenty, thirty, forty feet? What was the still unmoving, silent gunman up to? Ben wanted to look back, but didn't. That could be the trigger. Still his mount continued its sturdy walk, and the silence continued.

He was so drained he had to grip the horn to keep him from falling sideways from the saddle. But now he couldn't bear the strain of not knowing what was happening behind him, and he stopped and took a look back.

Miles was still standing there; the fires from upriver, just creating his silhouette with the shotgun now lowered at his side. The distance was nearly fifty yards, but Ben was certain he could see the man's impenetrable expression.

He wanted to lift a hand in

recognition, a tacit rite of clemency. Instead, he put the mare into a trot. For a long while he attempted to think out Miles's strategy but got nowhere. *Pity the rebs didn't adopt a similar stance at Missionary Ridge. It would have saved a few lives*, he thought wryly.

Several hundred yards below at a sharp bend in the road, Harry Gedding was waiting for him.

'It looks like the river's on fire further up,' Gedding said elatedly, as Ben rode up. 'They must be throwin' the stuff in.'

'That's exactly what they're doing,' Ben replied dully. He glanced out at the dark oily shapes of the timber as it turned and twisted in its course between the rocky banks. The canyon walls were still lit, and sparks flew high to the rims. But with his thoughts still on Miles, Ben was only part thoughtful of the display, was still shaky with nervous tension.

'I met up with Otto Miles,' he said quietly. 'He was waiting back there.'

'Miles? That makes it all the better

then,' Gedding responded.

'He stood in the road, and let me ride on.'

Gedding thought for a moment. 'Then it couldn't have been Miles you saw. Or maybe he knew I was out there in the dark,' he said.

Ben shook his head. 'Oh no, it was him. He'd already let you through. It was very strange, as though he changed his mind. So if there ever comes a time, you remember that, Harry. He let us both go.'

There was something in Ben's voice that shaped Gedding's response. 'OK, I'll remember, if that's what you want,' he conceded. 'That an' a few other things.'

It was after many more turnings along the deep-walled road before Gedding spoke again. 'Well, I reckon it was all worth it,' he said. 'They've already lost a darn sight more'n we did.'

'So have you thought about what comes next, Harry?' Ben responded.

'You've just reasoned why there'll be one.'

Gedding shrugged. 'Not yet. Have you?'

Ben didn't have to consider. 'I'd look for a man with eyes in the back of his head, arm him with a scatter-gun, and keep him out front at all times,' he said. 'Meantime, we go looking elsewhere for business.'

Gedding gave a short chuckle. 'You're your brother's brother alright,' he replied. 'How sure are you, about what happened to him, Ben?'

'Ninety per cent. Doc King an' Jesse both hinted at the same thing.'

Gedding let their thoughtful silence run for a long minute. 'You know, the doc said somethin' at the inquest about there bein' a doubt over the cause o' death. Reckoned Jesse took a bad crack to the head. Most folk assumed he'd probably *fallen* before the river got into him.'

'How do you mean?'

'It was at night, an' Jesse was drivin'

a rig. He wouldn't have been the first to have nodded off an' lost his balance. Above this stretch o' road there's any number o' places that hangs over the water.'

'There must have been something for the doc to doubt how he died,' Ben proposed. 'Maybe all those snakes put their poison into the doc to stop him telling what he knew about Jesse.'

'Ah, Ben, that's wild talk,' Gedding started. 'Miss Willow said her pa was in plain sight of a Chisel Canyon rail crew. Two of 'em got there quick . . . stood shootin' moccasins for ten minutes.'

'I don't doubt that. But why was he really up there?'

'It was his way o' relaxin' apparently. For some it's cards, for others it's the red end o' town. For Doc King, it was lookin' for herbs.'

'Hmm,' Ben muttered dubiously. 'Talking of Miss Willow; if Billy improves, she'll be wanting to return to town tonight.'

'Yeah, that's what she said she'd do.

Nate can take her the long way round.'

'I'll save him the trouble,' Ben said. 'Right now, Harpers Gap is where *I'm* supposed to be.'

'Still diggin' on Jesse?' Gedding said with a sombre shake of his head. 'You'll not find much, Ben. He made friends, not enemies. Could it have been someone he knew before he came here, an' they caught up with him?'

Ben considered what Gedding had suggested. 'He did write me about some trouble catching up with him. So yes, maybe that's it . . . maybe they did,' he said.

Half an hour later, the two riders saw the glimmering lights of Harpers Gap.

12

They found Billy asleep in the bunkhouse. All the crew except Nate Cobb had taken their blankets to the barn.

'It's probably still got some warmth to it,' Gedding said drolly.

Willow King wanted to return to Harper's Gap that same night, and Ben had already decided he'd take her. She left a jar of salve for Billy's wounds and an envelope of sedative powder if he had much trouble sleeping. Gedding gave her a hand onto the buggy, then handed her a couple of Navajo blankets.

'Take these,' he said. 'It'll get cold up there in the passes.'

Willow thanked him, said she'd ride out the following day to change Billy's dressings.

'No need, miss. I'm sure between us we can keep him clean,' he offered.

Once beyond the company's yard fence, the roan set into a steady walk up the long grade that Billy had raced his wagon down.

'So, that's Silver Track Freight, the company you're now in business with?' Willow said after a few minutes.

Ben gave a grin she could barely make out in the darkness. 'That's right,' he said. 'But with reduced circumstances since I joined up.'

'Why do you think it was Royston Poole who raised the fire?'

'He wanted to buy the yard. Harry and Jesse wouldn't sell.'

'Well he wouldn't get much by burning it down.'

'Yes, that's more or less what Harry thought,' Ben said. 'But he didn't burn it down, did he? I reckon it was a warning.' Ben continued with Gedding's assertion that Poole wanted a monopoly in the tie business, and Willow listened.

'I can't believe that. You make him sound like some sort of blackguard,' she bristled when Ben had finished. 'Roy's made his money and reputation out of honest businesses. Besides, you actually haven't a shred of evidence to back it up.'

Ben wondered what she'd say if she knew the Twin Rivers Railroad Company had hired him to watch her worthy Roy Poole. 'By the look of those stars up there, it must be close to midnight,' he said, evasively.

'Don't change the subject,' she railed. 'Next thing you'll be accusin' him of killing your brother.'

'No, I'm not accusing him of that,' Ben drawled seriously. 'I don't believe Jesse's death had anything to do with what happened today.'

Willow went quiet, pulled the blankets around her and leaned against the seat back. She was asleep, had been for nearly half an hour, when the glowing embers of Poole's tie-camp emerged from the canyon's wrapped darkness. She was sitting so close against Ben's right side that he gave a tight, uneasy smile at the thought of how he'd explain if she was wakened by him groping for his Colt.

As the roan walked the buggy on through the camp, a shack door opened and flooded the road with a yellow wash of lamplight. A man with a carbine cradled in the crook of his arm stood there looking out. Ben raised a hand in silent greeting, and the man nodded, acknowledged the silence as the buggy rolled on through the wedge of light. Then the door closed slowly and, knowing he wasn't going to be challenged, Ben breathed a sigh of relief. He wasn't wanting to explain anything to Willow.

Later, the Dirt Creek camp was also deep in slumber as the buggy rolled through. The road got rougher for a long stretch as it climbed beyond the camp, and Willow stirred. She woke, blinked, looked at Ben and dropped her head again. As time passed, Ben was thinking she'd returned to sleep, when she suddenly spoke out.

'How can you be going into business,

if you're still in the Army?' she asked.

Ben was glad of the opportunity to tell her, to have something different to say. He told of her father's letter and Noel Bonnie's refusal to grant him leave, of Eady and the doubts that had been nagging him for the past week. And then it was too late. He realized he'd broken the habit of keeping his innermost thoughts strictly to himself.

Willow put a couple of considerate questions to him, and whatever reserve he still held, Ben set aside before her openness and concern. He talked easily, found himself wanting her to understand why he'd acted the way he had. But eventually he lost the meaning of why they were talking that way, or that he could be part of such a private and personal search.

It was twenty minutes short of four in the morning, and the moon was a silvery crescent over the far peaks of the Crazy Bull Mountains, when the buggy rolled into the main street of Harpers Gap. A wintry bite was clipping the air

119

as Ben reined in before the King house.

Willow looked watchfully about her as he offered her a hand down. 'Thank you, Ben. You put yourself to a lot of trouble for me,' she said. 'You needn't come in.'

Ben smiled, understood the wary look. 'Thank *you*,' he responded. 'With not being a doctor and on such a bleak night. I'm just back where I came from.' He waited while she went up the front path and opened the door. The shadows under the porch roof were too deep for him to be sure, but he thought she hesitated for a moment, turned and looked back at him before pushing the door to. Goddamnit, she's changed her mind, he thought, but she hadn't.

Taking the buggy back on down the street towards the boarding house, Ben felt the tiredness piling into him. He closed his eyes for a moment, disappointed that the night time ride was over.

* * *

Later that morning, Eady Bonnie was unpacking her big valise, when the expected knock came on her door. She took a deep breath as she walked slowly across the room, attempting to ease away her irritation over Ben's absence.

'You've got some explaining to do,' she said as Ben stood guiltily in the doorway.

'I know,' he said quickly. 'I got caught up in the hills on business, and didn't get back much before dawn,' he said, using as much truth as he thought necessary. 'I've got something to tell you, Eady.' He indicated that she sit down. 'I've done some thinking too.'

As she took the chair, Eady couldn't understand his improved mood as she looked up at him. 'It must be good news,' she suggested.

'Just hear me out.'

Eady nodded. 'Yes, OK,' she said, sensing she wasn't going to like what Ben had to say.

'This business of Jesse's — well it's quite an outfit,' he began tentatively.

121

'It's well-established and makes money. Harry Gedding, Jesse's partner, is a straightforward feller and easy to get on with.'

Eady understood the line he was taking now, started to dread what she knew was coming. 'Go on,' she said.

'Twin Rivers and Yellowstone are both building through this country, and they're hauling all their materials and supplies into the hills by wagon. That's tons of everything. Everything from anvils and hammers to tobacco and candy. For a few years, this country's going to be seventh heaven for a freighter.'

'And?'

Ben's eyes gleamed with enthusiasm. 'Gedding needs a partner, Eady, so I'd like to take over Jesse's half of the business,' he said, dragging on the whole truth.

'Is that all?' she asked trying not to show the stabbing dread that cut straight through her.

'That's our big chance, Eady. A few

years from now you'll have everything you want. I even know of a house that's coming vacant soon, and we could make it to Rock Springs every month or so,' he continued, not noticing the telling drain of the colour from her face. 'How does that stack against another two years of cabin quarters . . . blizzards in winter, and guarding sodbusters in summer? Here, we'd have just about everything we need.'

It was a short, but awkward moment before Eady murmured. 'You're not too interested in resurrecting your career then.'

It was more of a remark than a question, and its starkness gave Ben his first inkling of Eady's real feelings. 'I'd probably have to do three months in the guard-house first,' he tendered warily, without humour.

She turned away to look out the window. Ben saw her knuckles go white as she clenched her hands.

'What have I said you don't like?' he asked. 'Is it about me or you?'

'*You*, Ben. You're just so full of surprises. Yesterday it was one thing, today it's another. I don't know where I am.'

'But I do. *Today* I know what I didn't *yesterday*. It's our chance, Eady. You and me together, starting over.'

Eady was suddenly dealing with too much, and she responded with an insensible smile.

Ben nodded, and pulled his hat back on. 'There's something I've go to do,' he said. 'You'll know what to say sure enough, when I'm back.'

Eady got to her feet, stood staring out the window. *Got to make a choice*, she thought. *Settle in penury, or go find Royston Poole.*

13

Fortunately, Eady didn't have to go looking for Poole. Later in the day, after returning from the upper canyon, he sent a message requesting that she meet him in the boarding house's sitting room. In the light of Ben Jody's part in the firing of his tie camp, he was keen to discuss her proposal, saw their meeting as a way to help him get what he wanted. *Two for the price of one*, he thought, grinning as he waited.

Seated as they were the previous night, he started by giving Eady an outline of developments in the railroad war, how a lot of his time was being taken up. 'We've got both companies laying hell-for-leather towards Windhammer,' he said. 'It's taking up more of my time than I'd want. Still, they're my concerns, and I had a thought or two about your Captain Ben Jody . . . *who* incidentally, was up the canyon yesterday.'

'Oh was he?' Eady responded, genuinely surprised. 'So what *were* your thoughts, Mr Poole.'

'To be effective, I need the help of the sheriff.'

'The sheriff? I wanted our arrangement to be confidential,' Eady said.

'It will be. Believe me, I couldn't afford to involve him if he wasn't trustworthy.'

'Why do you need him?'

'Well, there's a fair bounty for picking up army deserters, and most sheriffs are underpaid.'

'Ben's not a *deserter*,' Eady protested.

'No, I know that, but can he prove it? He's not carrying papers to say he resigned his commission, is he?'

Eady thought for a moment, then shook her head. 'No. My pa wouldn't accept it.'

'That's what I thought. So, suppose I let on to the sheriff that, through my acquaintance with you, I've learned that Captain Ben Jody *actually is* a deserter . . . something you let slip. Rather than let him put up a defence when he's arrested, we anticipate what he'd do.'

Eady was more interested now. 'What *would* he do?' she wondered.

'Send a telegraph to his post, probably. Which is exactly what we wouldn't want.'

'What's the sheriff's part?'

'I'll suggest he writes to the army post, asking if Ben has resigned.'

'And with Pa holding his resignation, they'll say *no*. But what happens to him?' Eady wondered, the fascination waning slightly.

'We're in luck right now, because the sheriff's away on business, and the deputy's in charge. He's a man who likes to keep out of trouble, but he'll want to get Ben to Fort Peck.'

'Where's that? I haven't heard of it.'

'It's one of the army's correction camps up near the lake. Far enough to keep Ben well out of sight. You'll have to wire your father, tell him something of what we're doing. Tell him you've found a way of getting Ben in line, but he'll need to support the desertion story when he's contacted.'

Eady was alarmed. 'We'll be getting Ben into even deeper trouble.'

'No, they won't want to keep an officer at Fort Peck. They'll return him to his post as soon as possible,' Poole explained. 'Once he's back, it'll be up to your father to do whatever he has to.' Poole took on a broad, knowing smile. 'I assume he'll be wanting to keep his son-in-law's record squeaky clean.'

For a long moment, Eady sat in silence, trying to see any flaws in Poole's proposal. 'Do you know how Ben would react if he learns that I've been involved in this, any of it?' she asked with genuine concern.

'I can imagine, Miss Bonnie. But if there's any questions ever asked, you just say I lied about what it was you told me.' Poole nodded across the room in the direction of the lobby. 'There's a few folk who've seen us talking together, but they won't know why, or what about. Much to their disappointment, I'll wager.'

'Yes,' Eady murmured. 'I suppose you're right.' Then she gave him a considering look. 'Why are you doing this?' she asked. 'I can't believe the age of chivalry is alive and kicking in Harpers Gap.'

'No, it's not,' he chuckled softly. 'Do you remember me saying I'd made Ben Jody a business proposition? That he turned me down?'

Eady nodded. 'Yes. You told me yesterday.'

'Well, your captain's just bought himself into a freighting company up at Swimfish. All of a sudden, he's become my competitor. So I see what I'm proposing as hindering competition at the same time as helping a lady.'

Slowly, Eady smiled. 'Fair enough. That's a gallant way of putting it.'

'Huh, gallantry has little to do with it, I assure you,' Poole said. 'Now I'd better go and put a word in one of Whitey Trigg's shell-likes.'

★ ★ ★

Grey cloud hugged the distant mountains until finally, with first dark, they settled on the upper foothills, then low over the town. The first drops of rain pelted the shingles of Royston Poole's office at his lumber yard.

'What, so you refuse to do it?' he said to Otto Miles.

'You don't pay me for that sort o' stuff.' Miles's voice was neutral. He wasn't afraid of Poole and didn't break his even stare.

Poole turned himself from side to side in his swivel chair as he regarded his man. 'You've got principles. Is that it, Otto?' he said with a chilly smile.

'Oh yeah, I've got 'em. It's just that they ain't always topside,' Miles returned and went straight out through the open door.

Poole stopped smiling. He had a few

pensive moments as Miles walked off, thought he might not have an accurate estimate of the man. Five minutes later, he took a bright yellow slicker from a hook beside the door and made his way to the far side of the yard.

The old wheel horse who'd been watching the rain, pushed against the slatted door of the feed shed. 'Do somethin' for you, Mr Poole?' he asked before Poole got close.

'Yeah. If you can wrest yourself from that snake pit, go and find Bast. Try the Black Robe first,' he said and tossed a half dollar to the oldster. 'This is for getting wet, and don't spend it until you've told him I want to see him. You understand, you old hay bale?'

'Yep, I understand Mr Poole.' The man sniffed loudly, spat out into the rain and tugged at the brim of his slouch hat.

Sheltering under the spread of a lone cottonwood, Poole hung around the yard for a while. Presently, with his mind made up, he ducked through the rails of the back fence, and walked in to town. He cut through a couple of small, cross streets until he approached the newly-built courthouse buildings.

There was a light in the window of the sheriff's office, and when he entered, Whitey Trigg was adding a key to a big ring before hanging it on a peg behind the desk.

'Another horse bolted?' Poole joshed.

Trigg didn't appreciate the humour, simply let a harassed expression settle across his already pinched features. 'Just puttin' it with all the rest,' he explained, jerking a thumb towards the iron-strapped jail door. 'He's safe enough in there, Mr Poole, but he don't look like no army deserter to me.'

'Yeah, that's the secret of success,' Poole replied agreeably. 'But you know what the telegraph said.'

'There could be some mistake.'

'I doubt it. But if there is, it's not yours, Whitey,' Poole said. 'You didn't let on about me being in on it, did you?'

'No. But he's asked a hundred times

where the allegation's come from.'

'Let him keep asking. When are you taking him over to Fort Peck?'

'Tonight after I've had supper. Can't I leave it till mornin'?'

'I wouldn't. Sheriff'll be on you like tick fever, if you hang around.'

'He will at that,' the deputy said ruefully. 'Just as long as it's me who gets the fat share o' the bounty.'

Poole dragged off his slicker and tossed it beside the door. Trigg sat on the corner of his desk, and Poole walked slowly around him.

'I need your help, Whitey,' he said.

'Can't remember too many folk askin' for that, Mr Poole,' Trigg replied, somewhat flattered.

'Perhaps they don't see what I do,' Poole said, keeping with the smooth talk.

'What can I help you with?' the deputy inquired.

'Suppose you discovered there was a dodger out on a man who worked for you. What would you do?'

'Huh, that's a double supposin' there, Mr Poole,' Trigg answered. 'But I guess I'd have to turn him in. Me bein' a deputy an' all.'

'Yeah. But what if he was a man you really couldn't afford to lose.'

'A man with his face on a dodger sounds like someone you're best rid of,' Trigg drawled.

'Let me put it another way, Whitey,' Poole suggested. 'Wouldn't the law have something to say about not turning such a man in?'

'Yeah it sure would. Know him, do I? This man you're talkin about.'

Poole nodded. 'It's Otto.'

14

Whitey Trigg's jaw dropped with surprise. 'Your Otto? Otto Miles?'

'Yeah, him,' Poole confirmed. 'There was three or four of them, and it happened a good ways south of here. I want you to leaf through some papers to see if there's anything about it. Can you do that, Whitey?'

'Yeah. If they sent it, we got it,' the deputy said and eased off the desk to pull open the bottom drawer of a filing cabinet. He lifted out a thick manila folder and brought it back to the desk. 'Sheriff saves all the circuit stuff that comes in. When would it have been?' he asked.

'I'm not sure. But if there's nothing there, forget what I've just said. We don't want to go branding a man who's done no wrong, do we?'

Trigg shook his head to agree they

didn't, and started thumbing through the assorted documents. There were Wanted notices for men whose descriptions were close matches, but it took a few minutes before Trigg showed Poole the actual likeness of Otto Miles.

When Poole was certain it was another copy of the poster he'd recently deposited at the bank, he asked Trigg to read the sparely-worded indictment.

''Otto Miles Meade. Suspected of Murder', it says. Miles is his *middle* name, here. There ain't much else.'

'Don't need to be. It's Otto, goddamnit,' Poole exclaimed.

'Yeah. It also says, he's of unkempt appearance . . . favours a blanket coat.' Trigg was looking worried now. 'What am I supposed to do? I'm ridin' solo an' there's Jody to take care of.'

Poole shrugged. 'You're the law, Whitey. Maybe he'll hear the owl hoot before you get back from Fort Peck.'

'Why should he? Why should he be any the wiser? From what you said, he's too good a man to lose. So, in the meantime, why don't *you* look out for him, Mr Poole?'

'How do you propose I do that?'

Trigg took his turn to shrug. 'If Welshbone was here, he'd swear you in, then arrest you if you didn't do what he charged you to do.'

Poole's look turned flinty. 'You've got hidden depths, Whitey,' he said. 'It seems I'm doing a lot of underestimating lately.'

'Yeah, well, that's as maybe, Mr Poole. But right now, an' for a brace o' reasons, I'd say it was in your interest to keep on the right side o' my deputy's badge,' Trigg suggested.

Muttering tetchily, Poole walked over to pick up his poncho. For a moment he watched the water drips hitting the floor, then he pulled it over his head. 'I'll have someone keep an eye on him,' he grated. 'But I'm not getting involved if there's any trouble. Is that clear, Deputy?'

'Very,' Trigg responded, seriously. 'But there'll be plenty if he gets away.'

Trigg was worried, and when Poole had gone, he spent ten minutes pondering on his predicament. Eventually, on deciding not to worry about what might happen to Otto Miles while he was away, he went to the Chop House for his supper, ate a better meal than usual at the thought of collecting a second reward. For some inexplicable reason, he also spent twenty five cents more than the county allowed for the meal he took back for Ben Jody.

★   ★   ★

A few minutes before eight o'clock, a well-used, rickety Concord stage splashed alongside the raised boardwalk in front of the courthouse. Without delay, Whitey Trigg led his prisoner out through the downpour.

'You order up this goddamn cloud seed just for me, Whitey?' the driver called down.

'Just enough to keep you damped down,' Trigg answered back as he slung aboard two carpet-bags. He secured Ben's handcuffs to the side strut of the forward-facing seat, then sat alongside him as the driver booted the brake forward and shouted for the team to move off.

The coach swayed into motion, gathered speed slowly with its four mules wary of the slippery footing.

Across the street from the court-house, a man who had seemingly been taking shelter from the rain, pulled up the collar of his duster and walked off towards the end of town. From the glow of the coach lanterns, he'd just been able to see how Trigg had restrained his prisoner to the seat.

Two hours after the stage had rumbled over the Milestone Bridge and swung north towards Fort Peck, Sam Paynter got to hear of Ben's arrest. He'd travelled to Harpers Gap that very afternoon, and the moment he heard the news, he went to find the Twin Rivers telegraph operator. Within minutes, the man was tapping out an abbreviated message to General Ambrose Quill in Rock Springs. *BJ arrested as deserter. Await instructions on RP surveillance*, the communication read.

★ ★ ★

At about the same time the telegrapher was turning out the lamp in the Twin Rivers office, Ben turned from looking out at the darkness to face Whitey Trigg.

'Why don't you take the seat over there?' he asked. 'I'd like to stretch out and grab some shuteye, even if *you* don't.'

Every so often, rain would gust against the curtain that Ben had fastened on his side. But through the open window at Trigg's corner, the glow from the coach lamp was just enough for Ben to see the deputy considering his suggestion.

'Yeah, might as well,' he replied. He thought for a moment longer before reaching for his Colt, then he handed the key to Ben and moved back into the corner. 'Be real careful. No one wants the paper work on a dead prisoner,' he warned, not bothering with the dry smile.

Ben unlocked the handcuffs, moved to the opposite seat and re-fastened them to the corresponding strut. Trigg leaned over and pulled at the fixing, tested it before pocketing the key and holstering his Colt.

'You must be pretty hard-up doing all this to collect army money,' Ben said casually. 'How much do they shell out for the likes of me?'

Trigg lifted his shoulders. 'Haven't asked. I guess it comes with the job.'

'Well I've got close to a hundred dollars that came with *my* job. It's yours if you'll turn me loose,' Ben offered but not quite as relaxed.

Trigg gave a thin, tolerant smile and shook his head.

Ben stretched, pushed his legs out and crooked his handcuffed arm for more comfort. 'At least you can tell me who turned me in,' he drawled.

'If I told you once, I've told you a hundred times already.'

'Yes, so you did. 'Someone who don't like traitors.' I suppose whoever that is, they won't be wanting half of the bounty?'

Giving Trigg something to ponder on, Ben closed his eyes. He tried to stop himself thinking about it because his thoughts always reverted to the same thing. Was it Harry Gedding, Willow King or Eady? All three knew how important it had been to keep his identity hidden, so he wasn't going to believe it was more than a slip of the tongue, a chance remark.

Instead of going over the deception once again, he thought about ways of leaving the stage before it got to Fort Peck. He guessed that at sometime during the long night, Trigg would be pressed by sleep and his vigilance would drop. All he'd need then would be a couple of seconds.

The swaying of the coach against its through-braces slackened now and he heard the teams slow to a walk. The sound of their hoofs was muffled by the rain as the road started up a steeply inclined mountain shoulder.

'Must be beyond Thousand Chains,' Trigg said, and reached into a pocket of his coat for something.

Ben was going to ask if that was where Twin Rivers had reached with their track laying, when the orange glow of the lamp was suddenly and completely blocked by a shadow. He was wondering how that could be, when a bright flash of powder flame stabbed in at the deep darkness of the coach — an ear splitting concussion that splintered the ash panels in a great crash of sound.

Trigg's shout was followed almost immediately by the driver's alarmed yelling. Ben was heaving violently against the handcuff's restraint when the shotgun exploded a second time.

Then there was a glow from the lamp again, and Ben saw the seat opposite him where the side-bracing had been completely shot through. The already tattered leather was shot apart, tufted horsehair was bursting through, and a dark stain marked the spot where Trigg had been seated. Now, the deputy's form was sprawled along the seat, indistinct and unmoving in the faint light. On the tail of the second shot, Ben heard a thump against the roof. The team bolted to the edge of the road, and with a vicious lurch the coach skewed and the ground dropped from under its wheels. It went over, and for the short moment it fell through a pit of blackness, Ben groaned in helplessness.

15

The old Concord took the force of a vertical ten-foot drop, squarely on its side. A rear wheel collapsed, the back boot brace cracked, and the top running rail buckled into the roof. The pair of lead mules were snapped from their traces and died instantly; the other two were thrashing wildly in their harnesses.

Ben was half-lying against the inside of the roof. Most of his weight was suspended by the handcuffs when the vehicle began to flip over. The double-tree fractured, and the flailing tongue struck one lunging animal, hurling it to the rocks far below.

The coach rolled for another complete turn before a jarring crash stopped it against the bole of a stunt pine. A splintered door pillar had raked the length of Ben's right arm, and he gasped at the searing pain. He rolled slowly to his knees, groaned as he lifted his arm to see the wound. Then he grinned in surprise when he realized the handcuffs had slipped from the side braces, were now dangling from his wrist. The broken vehicle shifted one final time then it settled, and only steady murmuring rain broke the overwhelming stillness.

Ben moved his seat, settled back against the panelling of the coach's front wall. He listened intently when he caught the sudden ring of an iron-shod hoof, guessed that one of the mules was still alive and trapped on the upper ledge. But a moment later he heard another sound, decided after a long, thoughtful minute it was the walking clip of the killer's horse.

He closed his eyes to concentrate his senses on the fading sound, realized his silence had kept him alive. After all, he was supposed to be a dead man. In a while his arm began to lose its initial numbness and he pulled a neckerchief from his hip pocket. One of his boots touched something with give, and he recoiled from Whitey Trigg's body. He took a few steadying breaths, decided he needed the key in the deputy's vest, then the Colt that was still rammed hard into its holster.

After releasing his handcuffs, Ben pulled the ammo belt from around the dead man's waist and pocketed a half-dozen extra shells. Then he thrust the gun into his own pants belt and tossed the empty holster into thorny brush beside the road.

He waited out the rain for fifteen minutes before cautiously pushing up against the coach door. Then he climbed out, found a solid footing in the rock and scree and hunkered down, listened for another minute. He wanted to light a match, but thought the flare would be too risky. He stood up, reached back into the coach, wondered what had happened to his skin coat as he pulled out a rolled poncho. Wrapping it tight against the gnawing dampness, he sat backed up to the Concord's mud-spattered underside and shivered with nervous fatigue.

He got to remembering the dull thump on the coach's roof, was in little doubt that the second shot was the driver being killed. He thought of finding out, but in the darkness, and not knowing how close he was to another drop-off, he daren't move.

Again, it was a sound from above that pricked his weary senses. Gripping the butt of the Colt, he sat up. With his nerves in flux, he held his breath until he realized it was the mule, and it was moving around up on the ledge. All of a sudden the remoteness wasn't so menacing and he hoped the animal wasn't badly hurt.

An interminable hour later, he opened his eyes against the soft, pre-dawn light. He realized he'd dozed off for a while, and the cold off the mountain had eaten into him. Shaking with the chill, he stood up, and with his right arm throbbing dully he stretched, turned his neck from side to side. The driver's lifeless body was half hidden by the stunt pine, spread-eagled in blow-down and loose scree. Ben took a break from a string of oaths and hexes to shed the poncho, then he started warily up to the line of timber.

Standing on the ledge, he ground his jaw in anger at what confronted him. Both the lead mules lay dead, their bodies twisted, necks broken. There was no sign of the third, but the fourth was standing with a snapped harness, its head was drooped, and reins trailed from its bit. He looked back into the canyon, didn't think anyone would believe a man had walked away from the smashed remains of the Concord.

'One day you're in for a real surprise. Whoever you are,' he rasped. He thought about Whitey Trigg and the driver, wondered whether he should climb back down, try to cover their bodies with rocks. But he wanted someone to find them, to see the fatal wreckage. Meantime, he'd be a dead man to everyone but Harry Gedding and Eady. He'd yet to make his mind up about Willow King.

Beyond and to the right of the animals, Ben saw there was a way up from the ledge to the mountain shoulder and with his meagre trappings he set off with the mule.

It wasn't difficult for him to pick up the killer's tracks. The rain had washed out most of the sign, but where the man had stood with his horse, laying in wait for the stage, the markings were settled that much deeper. The man had gambled on the rain lasting, but it hadn't, and the tracks made when he'd ridden off were even more evident. Ben spat contemptuously, decided he wanted to know which way the man had gone. It was an odds-on certainty where he'd come *from*.

Before Ben's slow pace had carried him a quarter mile, early sunlight was starting to cap the timber on the canyon's far shoulder. He was hungry and cold, his arm was hurting bad again and he started to shiver. But ten minutes later when he turned along the eastern slope, he found the sunlight and rested, soaked up the warmth. He scraped some moss from the weather side of a flat stone, pushed it into the sleeve of his shirt, against the wound. 'Willow's pa would have been proud of this,' he said quietly.

From then on he kept the mule at a steady, brisk walk, stopping only now and then to scan the road to make sure the killer's tracks were still there. It was when the tracks actually disappeared that he turned and rode slowly back. For a hundred yards he found no tracks other than those of his mule, then he found the place he'd missed. It was where a run of water had washed across the road the previous night. Now it was a shallow puddle of muddied, confusing signs.

He dismounted when he thought the shoe prints that slanted out of the wash were from a different horse. They swung sharply from the road, went down the slope to join the track of the horse he'd been following.

He cursed as he led the mule off the road and down the shifting slope. A few minutes later, the sets of tracks came to the edge of a cut bank and his curiosity deepened. The earth was softer and the horse tracks were clear, but there was no sign of them going on in any direction.

Ben looked apprehensively around him. *Is there more than one of you? Are you still here?* he silently wondered.

He walked the mule a pace or two to one side, then dropped to his knees. He stared at the ground for a moment, then roll-pinched some of the loose, dark earth with the fingers of his left hand.

16

It was mid-morning, and Royston Poole's tie crew were working the upper stacks along the river, sorting the burned and unburned timber. A rider on his way up from the Swimfish trail brought them the news that Sheriff Tommy Welshbone had received some opportune information, and had returned to Harpers Gap earlier than expected. At first light, he had impounded several crates addressed to Sam Paynter. It was a consignment of arms and ammunition intended to go up canyon to the Twin Rivers guards.

There was one man however, who didn't appear to be that interested in the turn of events. He was leaning against the cook shack, casually tapping the barrel of a Winchester against his leg.

From a hundred yards down canyon, where he'd been hunkered out of sight,

Ben Jody had been watching.

Ben had been led straight to the camp by the sign left by the second rider he'd tracked down from the hills. He'd made a wide circle of the camp to see if the hoof-prints had gone on, but they hadn't, and he'd settled down to wait and watch. Ten minutes ago he'd seen the man with the rifle accompany Otto Miles from the shack out to a stack of wood near the corral. Well guarded, Miles had carried several arm-loads of wood into the kitchen lean-to before going back into the shack again by way of its rear door. Ben knew he wasn't preparing the cook fire for the crew's late breakfast. No, for some reason Miles was being held prisoner. 'Out here, getting locked up's an occupational risk,' he muttered derisively. Then he cursed and started walking.

The guard didn't have a direct line of sight, but Ben had made it to the near corner of the shack before kicking up a stone. The man wheeled around to see he'd been taken by surprise. He was staring into the barrel of Ben's Colt, before he'd time to swing up his rifle.

Ben shook his head quickly. 'It's not worth dying for,' he warned the man.

The man went very still. He'd been taken by surprise, and he banged the butt of the rifle into the ground.

'Come over here,' Ben said.

The man made no immediate move, but then he thought better of it and walked forward.

'Put the gun down and open up,' Ben told him as he approached from the other side of the door.

The man nodded and leaned the rifle against the wall, took a few moments to remove the padlock. As he swung the door open, Ben stepped up close, pressed the muzzle of his Colt firmly against the man's spine and pushed him forward into the shack.

Otto Miles was sitting on one of two benches that made up the simple furnishing of the room. When he saw Ben, his big hands lifted away from the table and two face-up poker hands. 'The man's sure got a way with him, hasn't he?' he said, smiling thinly at the guard.

Ben closed the door and leaned back against it. 'So where did you spend last night?' he asked.

A comprehending look broke across Miles's face. 'Not where you think I did,' he answered. 'Tell him,' he directed the guard.

The guard's eyes hadn't strayed from the Colt that was now hanging at Ben's side. 'He was right here,' he answered in a hollow voice.

'Explain,' Ben said after a moment's thought.

'Boss's orders,' the guard put in. 'None of us could figure it out. We was told to hold him here.'

'Poole? And he was here the whole night?' Ben persisted.

'From about eight.'

Ben's glance went back to Miles. 'Why would anyone want to lock you in here?' he asked him.

Miles gave a single shrug of his shoulders. 'Royston Poole ain't *anyone*. I told him I wouldn't do a certain job for him, so he's decided the law can have me.'

'Well, that only answers part of my question,' Ben said. 'Why would the law want you?'

'He's got somethin' on me. Huh, like he has on most folk around here. But it's my line that's run out,' Miles replied.

As if confirming something he already had in mind, Ben nodded. 'So if it wasn't you up in the hills, who was it?' Ben asked.

'How the hell would I know?'

'Well I think you'd know him. Who was the feller with you the night you jumped me?'

'Cameron Bast.'

'Well near midnight, it was him who shot up a stage I was taking a ride in,' Ben said flatly. 'He's dead now, along with the driver, an' Whitey Trigg. I reckon I was meant to be lying beside them.'

'I wouldn't know about that,' Miles said after a few quiet moments. 'There's been worse lawmen than Whitey. An' you say Bast's gone as well?'

'Yes. Not then, but later. This morning I backtracked to where someone had waited to blow the top of his head off. Him and his horse are buried under a cut bank.' There was a significant pause, before Ben added 'Can you take a guess at who might have done that?'

'Can *you?*' Miles drawled.

'I can tell you where he is, where he snuck back to. I followed his sign straight back here. So who showed up here early this morning?'

Miles looked back at Royston Poole's crew man, who nodded slowly.

'Only the boss,' he said thoughtfully.

Surprise held Ben wordless for a moment. 'Where is he now?' he asked.

'Back in town, probably,' Miles answered.

'With a fresh mount?'

'Yeah, an' a top waddy's breakfast inside him.'

'You reckon he'd cut me down

because I put a taper to this layout?' Ben believed what he'd been told, but he was puzzled. What was Poole up to? 'He'd risk murder for that?' he put forward.

'Yeah maybe,' Miles said grimly. 'If I had an answer to half o' the whys an' wherefores, I doubt I'd be in this mess.'

Ben's thoughts were now getting more jumbled. He looked thoughtfully at his Colt, before thrusting it back in his belt. 'That's it? That's all you can tell me?'

'Hell, ain't it enough? You've heard that attack's the best sort of defence.'

'Yes, I've heard it. I knew a general once who *did* it,' Ben said. 'Maybe I'll let Sheriff Welshbone take a hand.' He eased away from the door and opened it. 'There's a rifle out there that I'll be taking. You give me two minutes, then I'll cover you while you make a run for it.'

Miles looked down at the hand of cards, at the high straight. 'It's all to do with timin',' he said abstractedly. 'Why would you do that?' he added quietly.

'I owe you.'

Miles shook his head. 'If you mean the other night, you had nothin' to do with it. Well, almost nothin'.'

Very little of what was being said, made sense to Ben. He watched as Miles had another glance at his unplayed hand.

'I killed a man. That's what Poole's got on me,' the man said simply. 'Unless you're a natural killer, you don't easy forget a thing like that. It sneaks up on you at the damndest o' times.'

Ben thought maybe he was understanding a little more and nodded.

'Like the other night. I couldn't pull those triggers,' Miles continued. 'I guess I was thinkin' how you had the chance to rearrange my face, and didn't. But Royston Poole would've done. He's different.'

'I know. He's a mean son-of-a-bitch, and he sold out the Twin Rivers on his last contract,' Ben said. 'Do you reckon he'll do it again?'

Miles traced a forefinger across the cards. 'I guess. He certainly won't have put the idea to bed.' He raised his eyes to Ben for impact. 'There's somethin' bad happening in that man's mind, Jody. You go find him. If not, he'll find you an' finish whatever it is he's started.'

'You really can't think of a reason?' Ben asked.

'Poole don't need one. For chris'sake, what's he had against some o' the others, proves that. What had Chayne done to him?'

'Jesse Chayne?' Ben cut in, his eyes suddenly flinty. 'What do you know about that?'

Miles shrugged. 'Not much. I was with him the night Chayne went missin'. We'd met him — Chayne that is — up the road here, eight or ten miles above. He was drivin' a wagon back to the yard. Poole's been after it an' was makin' a final offer. I got tired o' listenin' and drifted on ahead.'

'Go on,' Ben said, almost dreading what was to come, what Miles was about to tell him.

Miles shook his head. 'That's it. I was on the way back to town, goin' slow for Poole to catch me up, but he never did. The next day they fished Chayne out o' the river.'

17

In the early evening, Willow King walked along the side path of the house. She entered the office, was closing the door of the gloomy room when the rocker chair dipped and turned to face her.

'Hello,' Ben Jody said, evenly.

'Ben,' she stated after a short breath of relief. 'So you did get away.'

Ben lifted his arm, and showed her the torn, dark-stained sleeve. 'Yes, and just slightly scathed.'

Willow set her marketing basket aside. She crossed the shadowed room to a cabinet that was lined with shelves of shiny instruments and medicines. 'Take off your coat,' she told him as she peered into the cabinet.

Ben draped his coat around the back of the chair, then rolled his shirt sleeve high along his arm as he took a step towards her.

Willow turned to a sink beyond the cabinet and pumped a basin full of water. She soaped a clean rag and taking his wrist, began washing the dried blood from the swollen gash on his forearm.

'It's a nasty looking wound . . . could be infected. How did you get it?' she asked.

'Caught it on a piece of splintered wood.' Ben could tell immediately by the pressure of her touch that she didn't care much for his answer.

Willow dried the arm with a fresh towel, then took a bottle from the cabinet. First dark was well on its way, and the light was fading, but she could see well enough for what she was doing. She stained a wad of folded gauze with dark liquid, and quickly and efficiently swabbed the line of the long gash.

Ben knotted his fist and stiffened his arm. 'You're supposed to say it'll sting a bit,' he rasped as the sharp pain struck all the way to his shoulder.

With fleeting compassion in her eyes, Willow looked up. 'I'm sorry,' she said, throwing the gauze into the sink. 'I thought *you* were going to say something.'

'I did.'

'You know what I mean, Ben,' Willow flipped back. 'They've brought the bodies in, and some of them are still up there trying to find yours.'

Ben considered for the shortest moment. 'Are they saying I killed those men?'

'They are, yes.' Willow stood for a moment looking at him. Then she pointed to the table alongside the door. 'Why do you suppose I'm not lighting the lamp?'

'I did wonder. I thought you'd dabbed me with tanglefoot, by mistake.'

'I just don't want anyone to see you here. I'm afraid for you, Ben.'

'Well, thanks for that, Willow,' he drawled and meant it. 'But it won't be for the reason you're thinking.'

'What do you mean?'

Ben studied her shadowed face, tried to read the concern in her voice. 'How much does Royston Poole mean to you, Willow?' he asked soberly.

'Roy? He's a good friend. A good friend, nothing more. Why do you ask such a thing?'

'The other night you said he'd asked you to marry him.'

Willow nodded thoughtfully and affected a small worried smile. 'I'm not marrying him, Ben. I was angry at what you'd said. Does it matter?'

'Sort of. It makes what I'm about to say a tad easier.'

'Go on,' Willow said, the smile disappearing.

'Yesterday he somehow got to know about me resigning that commission. I don't know who told him. Do you remember we talked of it the other night?'

'Of course I remember. Are you suggesting it was me, Ben? After you saying you didn't want anyone to know. You think I told him?'

'No. But someone did,' Ben responded quickly. 'Him and me don't agree on ways to do business and he saw a way of hanging a desertion charge around my neck. He gets me out of the way and then . . . '

'And then *what*, Ben?' Willow cut in. 'How do you know it was Roy?' As she spoke she crossed the room, moved the rocker and sat in it by the window.

'Because I do, and it ties in with what happened last night. Let me tell you,' Ben continued. 'It was late, almost midnight, and we were on a stretch of road along one of the deep cuts. It was easy enough going; the driver might have been asleep for all I know. Then someone rode alongside and fired a load of buckshot through the window. Trigg was killed instantly. It would have caught me too, if I hadn't already changed to the other seat. He killed the driver next. Have you seen what a shotgun does to a man at close range, Willow?'

'I've seen the like,' Willow muttered in response. It was almost too quiet to be heard and she gritted her teeth.

'The horses bolted and we left the

road . . . fell partway into a canyon. The coach isn't fit for kindling, and I came out of it with this.' With that, Ben lifted his wounded arm.

Willow thought for a moment. 'Who could have done it?' she asked in a hushed voice.

'A man by the name of Bast . . . Cameron Bast. I followed his sign back down the road, but someone had been waiting for him. If anyone had gone looking, they wouldn't have found them where they'd been buried . . . him and his horse.'

'That's dreadful, Ben. So there was another man up there?'

'Yes, but Bast didn't know it. He was killed so he'd never talk.'

'Do you know who this man is . . . the other man?'

'That's where it goes wrong, Willow. He led me straight to Poole's tie camp, this side of Dirt Creek.'

'Yes, I know the place,' Willow nodded mutely. 'Go on and finish your story.'

'The person I thought of, was some-one who bore me a grudge an' likely wanted revenge. Only, he was under guard and locked up when I found him . . . had been since last night. He told me he was being held for the sheriff because him and Poole had a falling out.'

'Who was he?'

'Otto Miles.'

'I know him. A man of unprepossessing countenance.' Willow immediately held up her hand. 'I'm sorry, that was uncalled for. It's what came straight to mind.'

'To some it might,' Ben said with some irritation. 'But he couldn't have done it. That was down to whoever rode in there early this morning.'

In the significant moments that followed, Ben could hear the ticking of a clock from somewhere off in the house. He was wondering how to state the obvious, when Willow spoke.

'You're saying it was Roy,' she said.

Ben sighed and nodded. 'I know what I know, Willow, and that amounts to the same thing. There was no one else.'

Willow took a moment, looked down at her hands folded in her lap. 'I had a patient this morning who talked of little else but your arrest,' she started. 'He didn't know then what had happened of course, but he was a friend of Whitey Trigg's. It came as a bit of a shock when he told me that Ben Jody was an Army deserter.'

Willow paused a moment, her glance still directed downwards. Then she went on. 'I remembered your fiancée, her name, even. I got to thinking . . . wondering, and went to the . . . to see her. She was curious about me knowing you, but then I think she got some sort of respite from telling me. You know, a confidence shared.'

'What confidence?' Ben asked, when she said nothing more.

Slowly, Willow lifted her face. 'She said you really were a deserter. But she hadn't known it when she came here to meet you.'

Ben thought he saw a silvery glint in her eye, then maybe heard a tremor in her voice. He cursed inwardly, for a brief moment considered the extenuating story.

'And it's *you* that's listening to someone like Miles?' Willow's voice broke suddenly from its emotional low. '*You're* taking *his* word that Roy Poole has murdered three men in cold blood?'

'I believe *some* stuff I hear, Willow. The same as you do,' he added sharply. 'And it was only Bast, not three. And Jesse.'

'Your brother, Jesse?'

Ben nodded. He didn't say anything, but he knew then that one day he would probably have to kill Royston Poole.

'I need some time to think, Ben,' Willow offered. 'I think you should leave. It's getting late and — '

Willow stopped before she could say any more because they'd both heard the grate of foot steps from the gravelled walk. At the knock, Ben cursed quietly, and moved his hand towards the butt of his Colt. Willow saw the movement and gave an exasperating look as she rose from the chair, but she opened the door as though letting in a respite.

Against the fading light, stood a stocky, full-bearded man of middle years who reached up to tug the brim of his hat. 'I'm a bit pushed, Miss Willow, else I'd have got round to see you sooner,' he said hurriedly. 'This is the damndest thing that's happened in the Gap for some time. It should've been someone else, that's all I can say. There's plenty of choice . . . anyone but Cyrus.'

The man was obviously discomfited, ill at ease, and he touched his hat brim again. The movement of his hand brushed his coat open slightly, and Ben saw the gleam of a sheriff's star pinned to the vest underneath the coat.

'Won't you please take a moment, and come in?' Willow said, stepping back from the door.

'I'd like to, but not right now,' Thomas Welshbone said. 'I guess you heard about Whitey Trigg?'

Willow nodded.

'Yeah, darndest thing I've run into in a bunch o' moons,' the law man went on. 'If that feller's still up there, he's sure well hid. We've sniffed over that gulch better'n a tracker dog. I'll send out for Edge Cooter. He's someone who can trail worms.'

'Do you think whoever did it, got away?' Willow asked.

Welshbone shrugged. 'I'd like to know where he went if he did?' The lawman let his reply hang for a moment. 'Anyways, if there's the least thing I can do.'

'Yes, thank you Tommy. Goodnight.'

18

Willow stood looking along the path as Welshbone walked away. Then she turned, closed the door and leaning against it, looked wearily at Ben. 'You'll be needing a bandage,' she said quietly.

'It'll do as it is.' Ben rolled the sleeve of his shirt down over his bare arm, buttoned the sleeve and reached for his coat. 'Why didn't you insist on him coming in?' he asked.

Willow's gaze became more measured. 'Maybe I want to believe you. Maybe I need a bit more time. Where will you go from here?'

Ben took his hat from where he'd pegged it inside the door. 'To find Poole,' he said, turning to face her. 'After that, it's another day.'

Willow opened the door and stepped aside. 'Have you considered there not being one?' she levelled at him.

Halfway down the path, Ben held back the impulse to turn around. But he was up against a stack of twisted evidence. And now Willow had the sheriff's word against his, together with Poole's and Eady's.

Well it wasn't all bad, he thought. Only minutes ago, he'd seen that the doctor's daughter wasn't yet betraying her complete trust in him. And he knew by instinct, that Harry Gedding wouldn't. All of a sudden, finding Eady was more important than getting to Royston Poole.

★   ★   ★

Choosing the most darkened side to walk along, he turned from a cross-street to the Harpers Gap main street. When he came to the narrow stairway entrance leading up to the lobby of the Full Board, he went on past, then took a side-street. In deeper shadow, he paused a moment to look up to Eady's corner sitting room, where the shade of her window glowed with lamplight.

175

There was no one in the kitchen's entrance or the narrow hallway beyond, as Ben stepped in out of the alley. Halfway up the darkened stairway he stopped for a moment and listened, then he went on, turning at the head of the stairway along the dimly lit corridor above.

Eady's door was slightly ajar and a wedge of lamplight shone across the hallway's patterned carpet. Ben tapped, and from an adjoining room, Eady's voice answered.

'Come on in. It's open,' she called.

Ben stepped into the room, and, almost as an after-thought, closed the door behind him. When he turned, Eady was standing in the entrance to the bedroom. She was obviously surprised, and her face looked pale. She caught her breath, smoothed the front of her red velveteen dress, then brushed back a strand of hair from her forehead.

It was an unguarded moment that Ben had never seen before. 'It looks like you were expecting someone else, what with the door open an' all,' he said.

'No, no, it's not that, Ben. I was
. . . oh never mind.' Eady spoke quickly
but with uncertainty. She made an
effort to regain her composure, then
nodded to the couch along the near
wall. 'Come in and sit down,' she said.
She felt the impact of a steely glare, and
a bloom of colour rose quickly towards
her chin. 'I was about to begin dressing
for dinner,' she went on lamely. 'You
know, keeping up standards.'

Ben didn't move, but his brows lifted
in query as he wondered for who. 'What
time does the train leave, Eady?' he
asked with the barest trace of a smile.
'Or perhaps you could take the stage.
Now *that's* a style of travel that can be
real exciting,' he added drily.

Eady couldn't ignore the inference,
the barb of Ben's words. 'Very good. I
had that coming,' she conceded. 'It's
the night train and it leaves at nine.'

He nodded. 'Then you can talk while
you carry on packing. I deserve some
sort of explanation at the very least.'

177

'If you want. I could go tell them it was a fabrication. A . . . story gone wrong.'

'Gone wrong? You knew what Poole was doing?'

'Yes. We had a plan. What actually happened wasn't part of it though.' Eady's voice was losing a lot of it's timbre as she added, 'Father would have smoothed over everything.'

'So you believe it too?' Ben drawled. 'You believe I killed those men?'

'Didn't you?'

Ben smiled as he shook his head despondently. 'It doesn't matter either way now, Eady. But why didn't you tell Willow King the truth about me?'

At the mention of Willow's name, Eady bristled. 'Because she would have told everyone. She was meddling in something that wasn't her affair.'

'Maybe not her affair, Eady, but I doubt she would have told everyone. Besides, medical folk have a way of keeping things to themselves.'

For the shortest moment, Eady

appeared troubled and her eyes went a darker shade of grey. 'Do you really think she carries a thought for you, Ben? Something more?'

'I don't know. But if she does, I don't want it clouded by any falsehood from you,' Ben replied, disenchantment now touching his judgment.

'We're engaged. Have you forgotten, Ben? Why don't we start over? Come away with me now, buy your ticket on board the train.'

'There's one or two things keeping me here, Eady.'

'Well if you stay, that's it. I won't be twiddling my thumbs, waiting for you. I mean it, Ben.'

'Yeah I know you do. And I never did like ultimatums, Eady. And *I* mean *that*,' Ben said, and strode determinedly from the room.

19

Willow King felt completely worn out, and she stood by the office door for several minutes after Ben had gone. When her thoughts got her nowhere, she went to the kitchen and unpacked her marketing basket, but on seeing the eggs and chillies she decided she wasn't in the mood to eat. What she had to do was try and stop a confrontation between Ben and Royston Poole. Knowing where to look for Ben, she grabbed her coat and quickly left the house, making her way towards the Full Board.

Less than five minutes later, Royston Poole was turning his Surrey into the Harpers Gap main street. In fast fading light he recognized Willow, and slapped the team of chestnut mares to a smart trot.

'Hello Willow. This is a bit of luck,' he

called out as he slanted the vehicle in to the street's edge directly beyond her. 'I'm on my way to call on you.'

Willow was thankful for the near-darkness that hid her relief as she walked over to the buggy. 'I was taking a constitutional . . . ate rather too much omelette,' she lied.

'The moon's giving just enough light to show along the rim. Let me take you for a drive, instead,' he suggested in a friendly manner.

Wherever we go, it'll be away from Ben, was Willow's immediate thought. 'Yes, that would be nice,' she said.

After stepping down to offer Willow a hand, Poole climbed back aboard. He took the whip from its socket, and flicked it sharply to send the mares from their stand to a trot.

While they headed towards the outskirts of town, Willow speculated on Ben staying in town looking for Poole, when he knew he was being hunted.

As if reading her thoughts, Poole asked if she had heard the news of

Captain Jody. 'I wonder if he really was a captain? It looks like he pulled a lot of woolly stuff over our eyes,' he said, and chuckled softly.

'That's easily done if there's nothing to be suspicious of,' Willow answered. 'Do you think he killed those men?'

'It's possible. Question is, do any of us know whether he's *capable* of such a thing?'

Willow took a generous view on what Poole was saying, and with it, a small degree of reassurance. 'I've seen him,' she heard herself saying. And when Poole's head came round sharply, she wished she hadn't, but knew it was too late to change her mind.

'You've seen Jody? When?'

'Here in town, less than half an hour ago. There's some things that need to be said, Roy,' she said quietly.

Poole tightened the reins and the mares slowed to a walk. Ahead, Willow could see the first stretch of open country with the jagged line of the peaks still plain against the sky. She sensed his steady regard, and considered what to say. She controlled the impulse to ask him outright about all the accusations that Ben had made earlier, and it was several more moments before she spoke.

'He made some pretty strong accusations against you, Roy,' she started hesitantly, but turning to look him in the face.

'Well I wouldn't expect any billing and cooing,' he said with a thin smile. 'But what sort of accusations?'

'He said it was you doing the finger pointing about him being a deserter.'

'It was. I wanted him out of here, because he was getting tangled up in my affairs. What else?' he asked returning a stern glance.

'The other day I treated a man who was badly burned in a fire at the Silver Track freight yard,' she said calmly. 'This poor man — little more than a boy — said he saw you start it. Was he mistaken, Roy?' she asked more assertively.

'Of course he was. Heavens, why would I do such a thing, Willow?' He paused for a moment to think. 'But it makes sense as to why they burned me out,' he added.

'I don't understand.'

'An eye for an eye. The night my camp was fired, one of my men spotted Captain Jody. I know it's not quite the sort of treatment you're used to dealing with, Willow, but it's often the sort of medicine that has to be taken.'

Willow didn't know what to make of Poole's remark because Ben had made no mention of it; and she wondered why. Then she looked at the surrounding darkness, suddenly felt the press of isolation, the potential danger she was in. 'He accused you of other things, too,' she said, thinking that Poole wouldn't suddenly accept her silence.

'So, let's have them,' he said with a sharper edge to his voice.

'He said it was your man who shot up the stage last night and killed two men; that then you killed him to keep him from telling about it.' Willow felt her mouth drying, but risked truth against bluff or fabrication. 'And he's certain you killed his brother.'

'Whoa, you've turned too many pages,' Poole coughed out in surprise. 'Whose brother are you talking about?'

'His. Ben's.'

'I've never met anyone else by the name of Jody.'

'His brother's name was Chayne. Jesse Chayne.'

'The man I'm supposed to have killed?'

Willow stopped short of agreeing out loud, and nodded. 'Ben got the information from one of your men. Otto Miles,' she said.

'Ah, so that's how Miles got away?' he mused. 'Anything else from your good captain's report?'

'No, that was all.' Willow's voice was hardly above a whisper.

Poole gave her a quizzical look. He jerked the reins, hauling the mares to a stand. 'I can't believe you'd run the risk of coming out here with me alone, with no witness, if you actually believe any of that, Willow,' he said calmly.

'I'm telling you what Ben told me,' she said defensively. 'Are you going to shoot the messenger, or something to that effect?'

'The person you're talking about, would,' Poole replied smartly. 'Are you going to believe me, when I deny it?'

'You're giving me the best reason why I should.'

'Hmm. If I do decide to dispose of you, Willow, you'll be among the first to know,' he said with a deadpan smile.

Willow had no idea how much truth there was in what she was telling Poole. Quite how Ben could be right, and at the same time, Royston Poole not guilty of the things he stood accused of, she didn't know.

Poole grunted and sawed at the mares, turning and then slapping them impatiently with the reins.

'Where are we going?' Willow asked, fearful of a confrontation with Ben.

'To prove something. We'll drive to that goddamn stage to find the sheriff. That's where he was heading.'

Willow was going to say she had also seen Welshbone, but realized there was no immediate need. 'What help can he be?' she asked.

'Not much. But if I can get him back here and find Jody, we can settle this.'

The team settled into their swift, mile-eating pace, and it wasn't long before the road was beginning its gradual climb into the first of the foothills.

'You say Jesse Chayne was Jody's brother?' Poole asked.

'Yes,' Willow said, relieved at the likelihood of delay in Ben and Poole's encounter.

'I always reckoned there was something odd about him being found in the river that way,' Poole offered a few moments later.

'How do you mean, odd?'

'He'd been driving a wagon down to Fishtail. When it got late they were concerned at why he hadn't shown up,

187

and Harry Gedding sent a man out to look for him. They found the wagon off the road and the horses grazing. The next day they found Chayne in the river.'

'How do you know this, Roy?'

'I was at the inquest.'

Willow merely nodded and Poole continued. 'Otto Miles was at my camp in the canyon that night, so he could have run into Chayne. Maybe he knew Chayne before he came here, maybe there was some old trouble. If this Chayne wasn't using his real name, who knows?'

'Yes that could be,' Willow agreed because she knew that had also been Ben's take on the matter.

'Well it's of little consequence now,' he offered. 'Otto's going to be long gone.'

They had reached the crest of the rise and Poole urged the team to a faster trot. For the next quarter hour, and lost in their own thoughts, neither of them spoke against the steady drumming of the mare's run. Then, Poole reined abruptly from the well-worn ruts of the road to take a hardly visible set of wheel-tracks that branched off to the right.

'Where are we going, Roy?' Willow asked, her anxious voice breaking the silence.

'Don't worry,' Poole answered back as he drew in the reins. 'There's a couple of places where we have to make it through creek water, but going this way, we'll save time.' He stopped the mares and climbed down, took a few minutes to set and light the night lamps.

There was a warm, more friendly glow alongside them as they started off again. Although her momentary scare was waning, Willow's heart continued to thump against her chest. She leaned back against the seat, shivered and looked for a lap blanket that wasn't there. *How long will it take to find Ben, once we're back in Harpers Gap with the sheriff?* she wondered. What Poole had said about Otto Miles, took some of the sting from Ben's accusations. Ben had been deceived, of course, but maybe now she could consider the prospect of pouring oil on the troubled water.

20

Willow was still thinking about Ben Jody when a sudden jolt of the Surrey brought her senses sharp again. She peered ahead to see that they were headed down an incline so steep, that the horses were barely able to keep the vehicle from over-running them. Jack and stunt pine crowded close on either side, and rocks and loose scree, littered the slope. Close ahead, she saw the lamps reflected in a shimmering dark ribbon of water.

'Are you sure this is the right way?' she asked seconds later as the team splashed their way across a creek bed.

'It'll smooth out up above,' Poole said evasively, using the whip to get the horses up the far slope.

They crossed more even ground then, heading for a dark border of trees a half-mile beyond. They turned to run alongside, and after ten more minutes of smooth, fast going, angled deep into a fold of the hills. Another mile further on, Poole drew rein.

Willow stared uneasily into the darkness. 'You're lost,' she said, anxious and accusing. 'This isn't the way to where the stage was found. What's going on, Roy?'

'I did say you'd be the first to know,' he said with the same straight smile he'd delivered earlier.

'You're going to kill me. Is that it, Roy? Have you decided to get hanged for the sheep?'

'I said I'd dispose of you, Willow. Not kill you.'

In the lamplight, Willow watched Poole as he worked on the horses. 'How do you intend to do that?' she asked with a nervous laugh.

'By making you walk home. You'll get ruffled and short-winded, but you'll certainly live.'

'Live to tell the tale of what exactly's been happening up here,' she suggested drily. 'Ben was telling the truth, after all.'

Poole was unbuckling a breeching-strap on the offside mare. 'In just about everything,' he confirmed.

'But he lived while two other men died. Then you shot the killer you hired. You'd already killed Ben's brother,' she accused in a hushed voice.

'Cameron Bast wasn't the sort who's going to be missed, and as for Jesse Chayne, well, I haven't got where I am today by letting people like him get in my way,' Poole said. He was staring at her intently as he went on in a flat grating voice. 'By owning that freight outfit I could have called the tune, made them dance *and* get well paid for it. There would have been no limit. With the money they're throwing around up in that canyon, why shouldn't I take a share?'

Willow assumed it was a rhetorical question and she remained silent.

Poole shrugged and turned his back on her. 'That night, Chayne rejected my offer . . . scorned it, more precisely. I don't take to that sort of response, and with one thing leading to another, we had a fight that he lost. If your Captain Jody hadn't happened along, I reckon I could have won Harry Gedding over, and none of this would have happened.'

Willow shook her head in disbelief. She waited a moment and when she was sure Poole wasn't going to say anything more, she murmured. 'Pa had most of this guessed out.'

Poole nodded. 'Yeah, I know. If those at the inquest had listened to his diagnosis, I might have had to pull out sooner. I guessed he'd write Chayne's family . . . Jody's family.'

Willow watched as Poole stripped the harness from both horses. She noticed he was leaving their bridles on, and started to tremble.

'There's a wool rug on the back seat,' he said, sensing her predicament. 'You can curl up and sleep right here. Things never seem quite as bad in the morning, do they?'

'Why morning?' she said, her fear now tempered with cold anger. 'I'll start walking the moment you ride off.'

'This time of night's for wolves an' bears an' big cats, Willow. They don't take kindly to trespassers.' With that, Poole dropped the last length of harness and pulled himself up onto the back of one of the mares. Leading the second, he reined alongside the Surrey. 'Besides, when it's full light, you'll make it back to the road in quick time.'

The lamplight allowed him to see the disgust that blazed in Willow's eyes. 'I wish things could have turned out differently. You know, I'm only doing this because I love you,' he said, an ironic smile breaking up his rugged features. Then he reined his horse away and walked off into the darkness.

Willow didn't respond, she just watched until he disappeared. And when the stillness was utter and complete, a cold, resolute anger stirred deep inside her.

*　　*　　*

Regardless of not knowing where she was, or of Poole's warning of night predators, Willow had no intention of spending the night huddled in the Surrey.

She pulled one of the coach lamps from its bracket, took a look at the stars and started walking west. 'Come on Mr Cuffy,' she challenged, in a lowered voice. 'Now's your chance.'

After a long ten minutes with the damp already gnawing at her ankles, Willow had cautiously skirted a small clump of scrub pine and brush, when just beyond, and in its own little clearing, a stricken, uprooted juniper loomed out of the darkness. Its dead, grey-roots and ashen spiky branches rose through the tufts of grass, and beyond the reach of her lamp, its dried out trunk was darkly scarred where lightning had struck many years before. It was an eerie sight, and she was about to walk on when the thought struck her.

In the lamp-glow she could see nothing but high grass stretching away on all sides. She walked around the remains of the tree to make sure it was a good distance from the main stand of timber, then she thought of the men who must be somewhere along the higher road at the site of the wrecked stage.

Under the wedge of lamplight, Willow scuffed up some decayed twigs and with the side of a sodden boot, kicked them into the hollow under the roots. With one hand she added some dead bark and a few handfuls of dry needles. She started to prize open the back of the lamp, then had a more effective idea, something that better suited her frame of mind.

She took a step back and hurled the whole lamp as hard as she could, watching for a moment as the spilling coal oil seeped into the shrivelled roots and clots of dried earth. The flame burned slow and blue at first, after that yellow and red, as it took hold of the big old trunk. As the fire caught at the dead timber, Willow backed off. Within minutes, flames were leaping above the height of the thickets that skirted the blow-down, and Willow gasped at the sound and ferocity of the burning. A forest fire was a fearful incident in these richly timbered hills, and she hoped that from a distance and higher up, this one would be spotted by Sheriff Welshbone's men.

21

The four men Tommy Welshbone had left to search the canyon below the wrecked stage were drinking coffee beside the Windhammer road, when Edge Cooter came riding in on a big Jenny mule. The old scout was tired after his ride, and the others had to watch him sit for a while before he was ready to start his work.

'How much is known about all this?' he asked, wiping away tobacco juice and coffee from his whiskery chin.

'Not much,' one of them answered. He stepped over to the edge of the road with a lantern, holding it out as if the wreck could be seen below. 'No one was goin' to walk away from that.'

'There's no sign at all?' Cooter was thinking that maybe he'd rode many miles for nothing.

'A bit, down there. Someone waited

down there in the trees for the stage, then rode out alongside it. We reckon — '

'Huh, I know all that,' Cooter cut in. 'But what have you found since noon?'

'Nothin' more,' one of the others said.

Cooter shrugged irritably, then after a moment's sniffing, started picking his way warily down the slope. At the wreck, he started looking around, wanted to know exactly how Whitey Trigg and the driver had been found.

'An' what's this doin' here?' he said, lifting a poncho from the broken spoke of a wheel.

'It was up there,' a man said, pointing to the road above. 'Must have come down with the coach.'

Cooter turned the poncho inside out, saw the unmistakeable stain of blood on the inside. *Looks like the feller was hurt before he ended up down here, he thought. Takes one hell of a smart hombre to work that out,* he added sarcastically.

He was thinking much the same when they were up on the ledge, and when they showed him the prints of the killer's horse. He was sniffing and cursing the lantern's poor light, as he hunkered down in the middle of the road. He pointed to one set of tracks among the confusion of hoof marks in the hard-packed dirt.

'This was the bronco he rode away on,' he said.

'That *who* rode away on?'

'The man you're looking for. Whitey Trigg's prisoner.'

'Rode away?' one man questioned feebly. 'Hell's bells, we been down in that gulch lookin' for his body since noon.'

'Yeah, I'm sure,' Cooter drawled. 'The feller you want was hurt, but he managed to lead one o' them broncs up here from the crash. Hard to tell, the way you clod-hoppers have messed up the sign. But after the rain stopped, it looks like he took a look around, before ridin' off.'

'This first man, the one who stopped the stage. Could he have been a partner of the man we're after . . . Ben Jody?' someone asked quickly.

'Huh, Welshbone don't pay me enough to speculate,' the old scout answered caustically.

'Well, I'm not too certain for what, but we're obliged,' the man replied. 'You've just helped us put a rope round a man's neck.'

'That was down to him,' Cooter rasped. Within minutes, he was back on his mule and riding towards Windhammer.

Although there was plenty of time for what they had to do, Welshbone's men didn't waste much time making their return trail to Harpers Gap. But they had hardly covered the first winding downhill mile, when the rider ahead spotted a bright, red glow shining against the backdrop of the lower foothills. They drew rein and sat silently watching until the flames grew, began licking into the dark sky.

'What the hell's that?' one of them said.

'Well, it ain't no trapper's campfire, that's for sure,' someone answered.

'You reckon we should ride down there?'

'Yeah, some of us should. We could split up,' suggested another. 'I'll ride on to town.'

Not completely certain of their involvement or the general scheme of things, the men sat watching the flames for a minute. Then, three of them took a heading down through the pines, and the fourth man heeled his mount towards Harpers Gap.

'Give me a couple of hours,' he shouted.

* * *

Well after full dark, Royston Poole turned the chestnut mare in at the Harpers Gap livery corral. He didn't bother removing the animal's bridle before bringing down the gate pole and making off in the direction of the main street. When he'd gone, the horse just stood there with its head down. Its neck muscles were quivering and its heaving flanks were flecked with foam. It was worn out, too tired to move across to the water trough. Poole kept glancing furtively behind him, slowing each time he saw a figure in the darkness. He turned into an alleyway, edging along the clapboards until he came to a side door of the Badger Hole. He turned the handle and stepped cautiously into the low-lit, pungent atmosphere.

Edging through a murky poker bay, he nodded to a couple of acquaintances, smiled thinly at a girl wearing a petticoat dress and a pearly hair-pin in her blonde hair.

'You look good, Angie,' he said. 'Has Harve Munroe been in tonight?'

'He *was*,' she said. 'Are you staying?'

Poole shook his head and turned back to the door. 'I'd like to find the time,' he muttered.

The man Poole was looking for, was in another dog hole bar, further along the street, close to Carlo's Chop House.

He picked him out immediately, but had a good look around before approaching him.

'I want to talk to you,' he said, his eyes still quartering the room.

'Wantin' an' gettin's two different things, Mr Poole,' Harvey Munroe said tartly. 'We said all we had to, earlier.'

'Well I'm here to say it again. You won't regret it if you just hear me out,' Poole replied, and stepped back into the short hallway, that led off the bar.

The two men had already exchanged some heated words after Ben Jody's visit to the tie camp, and Otto Miles's escape. But a moment later, Munroe cursed resignedly, then picked up his glass of beer and followed Poole.

'It'll take more than just hearing you out, Mr Poole,' he offered directly.

'I've got margins to consider, Harve, but I can improve on what we talked about earlier,' Poole said when they were standing close.

Munroe brushed froth from his top lip. 'I offered five grand, if I recall,' he reminded Poole, dryly. 'That was for the mills an' the contract.'

'For ten, I'll throw in the camp . . . the river yard. How about it?'

'Huh, I hear that's mostly turned to charcoal.' Munroe smiled crookedly. 'Reminiscent of when you crowded me out.'

'Careful, feller. It sounds like there's an accusation somewhere in there. That's a wicked calumny,' Poole said, taken aback by someone suddenly standing up to him.

'But there's no one listenin'. It's five an' the contract,' Munroe offered, pushing for advantage.

Poole was going to try arguing again, but he knew time was running out, and Munroe was stubborn and aggrieved. 'OK, five thousand,' he ceded.

As if for a better look, Munroe leaned in, then took a half step backwards. 'You in some sort o' trouble?' he asked. But he quickly realized he wanted nothing more than the deal and he held up a hand.

Poole nodded. 'I'd have waited until tomorrow for ten, not for five. I want the money tonight.'

'I get that. But wantin' an' gettin's two different things. *Are* you in trouble?'

'I want to be out of this goddamn place, and up in Windhammer as soon as possible, OK?' Poole replied. 'Why the hell do you think I'm in here, sneaking around like a garbage rat?'

Munroe, shrugged. 'I dunno. Lost in a crowd, I guess.'

'Yeah, very funny. Listen, Harve, you know what's up. You're the only one who does. Now we made a deal, so just go get the money. Raise it if you have to. Your word's good enough for folk around here.'

It was less than a year since Munroe had taken a hammering from Poole, and been forced to sell him his business. Now he was settling the score. Along with four others, he was buying back his tie mill, a leased yard on the river, and a contract for countless thousands of cross ties. 'I'll collect it in nickels an' dimes if I have to,' he said, with a lean smirk of revenge. 'Where'll we meet?'

'My room at the Full Board in an hour. I'll have all the paperwork ready.'

'Just don't forget that contract.' Munroe pulled his coat together, buttoned it purposefully as he turned away.

22

Almost the first man Harry Gedding saw as he shouldered in through the bat-wing doors of the Black Robe was Nathaniel Cobb.

'Nate. You had any luck?' he asked, when he got close.

Cobb's immense fingers were toying with an empty shot glass of whiskey. 'No, none,' he said, raising his eyes to the back-bar mirror.

Gedding caught the barkeep's eye, reached out to stop a bottle and glass that shortly came sliding down to him. He filled his and Nate's glasses, emptied his at a gulp and re-filled it.

'I'd go easy on that stuff. It can drown your brain,' the blacksmith said, knowing that Gedding wasn't normally a drinking man.

Gedding had something on his mind and ignored the remark. 'Nate, think back. What was Ben at the yard for, this afternoon? What did he do?'

'First off, he asked for you.'

'Then what?'

'He jawed with young Billy for a few minutes. Told him to rest up for a few more days. Then he went into the office and wrote them letters I gave you. One for you, one for Sam Paynter.'

Gedding nodded. 'How do you reckon he knew Paynter?'

'No idea.'

'And he didn't say anything else?'

'Nope.'

Gedding drank half his second glass of whiskey. 'You said his arm was hurt?'

Nate looked directly at Gedding and nodded. 'Yeah. No doubt.'

'That's the bit that ain't good,' Gedding said, and drew in a long breath. 'Half the town would like to believe he did those killings, Nate.'

'Yeah, an' the other half already does. Well he ain't hid out in them places you said to look. But how about Doc King's kid? She might know somethin'.'

'She ain't exactly a kid, and yeah, she might. That's a good thought, Nate.' Gedding was already turning from the bar and heading for the door as he spoke.

As he hurried up the main street towards the King house, he cursed for confiding in his blacksmith. The brief note he'd received from Ben Jody, specifically asked him not to tell anyone that Royston Poole was implicated in the killings. *Huh, easier said than done,* he thought.

★ ★ ★

The front door of Doctor King's house was unlocked when Gedding tried it, but the only thing that answered him was the slow ticking of the long-case clock. He closed the door quietly, turned around, and went back up the street. Deciding to spend the night at the Full Board, he'd just passed a darkened store-front, when a voice called his name. It was Ben Jody.

211

'Goddamnit. Of all the places . . . ' was all Gedding could think to say as he hauled up short and took a deep breath.

'It's the best I could come up with,' Ben issued from the shadows. 'I thought I asked you to stay away, Harry.'

'That was this afternoon. I didn't know you meant all day. You know that most o' the folk in this town would go for a candle-lit hangin' if they could lay hands on you. What the hell are you playin' at?'

'Well, I got me a doorway out of harm's way and I can see both sides of the street. Besides, it's too early to turn in,' Ben said, and Gedding thought he sensed a wry smile.

'Have you seen anything o' Poole?' he asked, barely able to make out Ben's shape in the gloom. 'Is it him you're layin' for?'

'If I had seen him, he'd be dead.'

Gedding knew it was too late to change Ben's mind, but he tried. 'Look,

Ben,' he said, 'There's a lot o' water still passin' along the Musselshell, so are you that sure there ain't some other way?'

'Yeah, I'm that sure, Harry,' Ben replied. 'But thanks for your concern.'

Gedding was angered with worry. 'You've got a busted arm, for chris'sakes,' he flared. 'At least get the sheriff to go with you.'

'No, he'll know of some reason why I can't kill him. Of course, if *you* was to find him an' let me know, you'd save me a long wait.'

'Poole? Where'd you reckon he is?'

'Well, he must do a lot of business from somewhere here in town. If I knew where that was . . . '

'He's got some rooms at the Full Board,' Gedding said helpfully.

Ben quickly stepped out of the deeper shadow. 'Yeah, I know where that is. Thanks, Harry.'

Gedding groaned at the giveaway. He reached out and put a hand to Ben's chest, pushing him back into the doorway. 'I fell for that, Ben, but I'm the one who can walk in there, not you.' He didn't give Ben a chance to answer. Half-a-dozen strides along the walkway he looked back, but Ben wasn't following.

He climbed the steps to the boarding house lobby and went straight to the desk. 'I want to book a room. Meantime, I'd like to see Mr Poole. I hope he's in,' he said, confidently.

'Up the stairs. There's a two on the door,' the man replied after a moment's thought, trying to place the would-be guest.

As he crossed the lobby, Gedding cast a quick glance at the two couches that sat with their backs to him. Seeing they were empty, he headed on up to the rooms that Poole was occupying.

Gedding lowered his head, used the brim of his hat to conceal his face as a man approached him coming down the stairs.

'Coincidence or what eh, runnin' into you, Harry?' the man said, stopping beside him.

'Hi Harve. Guess I wasn't expectin' to see anyone I knew on these stairs,' Gedding replied, looking up and recognizing Harvey Munroe.

'Royston Poole's just sold me his layout. Well, sold it back, more accurately. But now it's the whole kit an' caboodle.'

'Sorry Harve, what are you talkin' about?' Gedding said, genuinely surprised.

'I've just bought him out for a two-bit price, tie contract an' all. Looks like you an' me's doin' business together, Harry.'

Gedding looked quickly up the stairway, and smiled. 'Well I guess in the face of that, my other business can wait, eh Harve?' he said enigmatically. Then he turned and went back down the steps.

'Were you goin' to you see Poole?' Munroe called out, but Gedding kept going.

★　★　★

215

Gedding left the building hurriedly and went on down the walkway. 'He's there all right,' he said when he got to the doorway where Ben was still waiting. 'An' he's certainly carryin' on some sort o' business.'

'Did you see . . . hear something?' Ben asked, moving from the shadows.

'Yeah. If you can believe it, I actually met a man on the stairs,' Gedding started, but without a smile. 'His name's Harvey Munroe, an' he told me Poole had just sold him everything. Weren't too concerned about top dollar, either.'

'He sold everything?'

'Yeah, the whole ball o' wax. Even the goodwill. Our Mr Poole sounds like a man who's short for this town.'

'Well, that changes everything, Harry,' Ben speculated. 'I think you've got to open that note I left for Sam Paynter.'

'I don't follow. How does *he* figure in this, Ben?'

'I'm working for Twin Rivers, Harry. It's Paynter who's paying me to keep an eye on Poole. You can add a postscript to what I've already written him. Say they'll be dealing with this new feller, Munroe, from now on. An' tell him to let General Bonnie know I've made contact.'

'Don't you think you should be doin' this yourself?' Gedding asked.

'Perhaps,' Ben said stepping out into the street. 'I know that desperate ills require desperate remedies,' he added, his nippy smile sliding into a grimace.

23

Lit by a single oil lamp above the dish tubs, the kitchen of the Full Board was very dark. The air was fusty, redolent of fried meat, and Ben didn't waste any time in getting through the room and across to the stairs.

A low murmur of voices drifted from the lobby, and for a moment he speculated on whether Eady had actually caught the train. Maybe she was in her cups, sitting with Poole wondering where it all went wrong. *Willow King wouldn't have tried that*, he thought.

Halfway up the stairs he straightened his bad arm, felt the stiffness when he flexed his fingers. But there was strength enough for a firm grip when he lifted the Colt clear of his belt. He realized he was holding his breath and trying to avoid the squeaking treads. *Stupid*, he thought as he climbed to the stairhead, *the man's not sitting there waiting for me.*

As he stepped into the low light of the upper hallway, he heard the click of a door closing just ahead of him. Then he saw a brass number on its upper panel, made out a 2, then a space where there was once another number.

'So, this is where you are?' he whispered to himself as he stood in front of the door. Then he gripped his Colt, took a breath and kicked it open.

The door's sharp back-swing jarred into something, and there was a startled curse. But Ben recognized it as Poole's voice, as he lunged into the room.

Powder-flame immediately scorched the back of his neck, and a thunderclap explosion deafened him. He threw himself sideways, lifting his injured arm towards the darkness from where the shot had come. But a numbing blow hammered him and the Colt went spinning from his hand. Instinctively, he brought his left arm swinging around in a desperate, savage blow. He connected, and Poole staggered into the wedge of meagre hall light.

Ben tried to knee the man in the groin, but Poole sensed something of what was coming and doubled over, taking the force of the blow in his stomach. His hands clawed open as the pain hit him and he dropped his gun. He stumbled towards it, kicking it somewhere across the room. Dazed, he staggered against Ben, gagging for breath from the violent knee-lift. He lowered his head, closing his arms closed around Ben's waist in a bear hug.

It drove the wind from Ben, who spread his boots and suddenly swung his upper body around. Poole was carried off balance, but his hold didn't break and they fell together out through the door.

Poole ducked his head, and when they hit the floor, the top of his skull drove up against Ben's chin. Ben gasped and lifted a boot, shoving against the wall. But before he had time to get to his feet, Poole twisted around and made a dive back at him.

Ben rolled to one side and put his arm out for support. But there was nothing there, and he realized too late that he'd reached the head of the stairway, was already falling. He tried to double up, pull his arms and legs in as he rolled down. The edge of one step caught a shoulder blade and a pain stabbed deep to his spine. His mind registered faraway sounds, then after what seemed an eternity, he piled up at the bottom of the stairs. He lay still for a short moment, waited for everything to stop banging and thumping, inside and out of his body.

Behind him, taking the steps two at a time, Poole came chasing. Ben went into a crouch, turned and saw the man almost on top of him. Poole shoved out a boot, and Ben dodged his head to get caught on his injured shoulder. The blow sent a shock wave through him, but Poole went on over him in a diving fall.

Ben rolled over slowly, in a daze heard someone shouting from the hallway above. And then he was

221

pushing to his feet, making for the main hallway when Poole hit him. It was a driving blow that connected high at the side of his head. He reached for the wall of the corridor, braced himself as he stood up, as Poole struck him once more low in the back above the kidneys.

Pain consumed Ben now as he stumbled around. He saw Poole's fist arcing towards his face and he ducked his head and shoved away from the wall. He drove two blows into Poole's stomach, fire streaked up his right arm and he delivered a wild kick at the man's shins.

'You're one hell of a mixer, Poole,' he grated. 'I'll give you that.'

Poole grunted and as he took a step backward, Ben realized he was beaten if he continued to fight this way. Poole would wear him down, then probably cripple him for good, if not worse. He recalled their first proper encounter, what Poole had said about officers. *This is the moment to think etiquette. Queensbury rules*, even, he told himself.

As Poole leant into his task and came

at him, Ben side-stepped, and with a tight grimace he jabbed with his left. Poole tried to brush the blow aside, and seeing the opening Ben threw his right up into the meat of Poole's face. The blow connected, Poole drew away and Ben ground his jaw in agony.

From the corner of his eye, Ben noticed the hallway was crowded with onlookers. Brought out by the crash of Poole's Colt, they had gathered at the lobby end, shocked and fascinated.

'The art of fisticuffs,' Ben rasped wearily as him and Poole circled each other. 'But I'd shoot you if I had a gun.'

Then, breathing heavy, Poole charged. He was flailing with less purpose now, and again Ben twisted aside. Poole went off his balance, and Ben hit him with a well-aimed fist to the temple. Poole was stunned, and with his head dipping, he reeled across the corridor towards the narrow window that overlooked the side-street. He grunted once, then turned to face Ben, who, considering for the short-est moment, drew back his arm and stepped forward. He met the man's frenzied eyes, then, with a mixture of fear and anger, pistoned his balled fist at the middle of Poole's big, ruddy face. He felt the crumple of knuckle and nose bones when his hand smashed home, but he watched in awe as Poole's heavy frame staggered backward into the window. The glass panes shattered and the sill caught the back of Poole's legs. Searching for the window frame, his arms windmilled and he tried to throw his head forward, desperate for some sort of balance. Then he gasped, stared back in silent astonishment and fell into the darkness.

'Profits come in by it, and justice flies out,' Ben said hoarsely and with deep cynicism.

★ ★ ★

Sheriff Welshbone had arrived at the boarding house in time to accompany Ben to the lobby.

'Get Alice to bring soap an' water,' he

barked at the clerk, but watching Ben as he eased himself onto one of the couches.

'There's some stuff o' yours in my office, son,' he said. 'A beaver coat an' a big ol' Army .44.'

Ben sat with his eyes closed. 'How's Poole?' he asked.

'You saved the county a few dollars in scaffold money,' Welshbone replied. 'Call in an' see me when you're passin'.'

There was a woolly jumble of voices then, but Ben didn't want to listen.

'I'll just clean your face up a bit,' a voice close to him said.

He opened his eyes and saw Willow King kneeling beside the couch. Then came a warm sting as she gently swabbed at his cuts and bruises.

'I know it wasn't about me this time,' she said.

'No, not this time, Willow,' he agreed wearily.

'He admitted it all, Ben. He took me clear to the foothills, then left me. If it wasn't for the sheriff's men, I don't —'

'Well I'm glad it came from him,' Ben interrupted. 'I wasn't that certain you believed me. Not completely, anyway.'

Willow stopped her ministrations. 'Is this the end of your troubles, Ben?' she asked, with more noticeable purpose.

'Oh I wouldn't go that far,' he said. 'It just confirms there's someone up at Duckwater who owes me a fat bonus — something in lieu of an Army Captain's pension.'

'So you won't be leaving Harpers Gap?' Willow asked in anticipation.

'Hell no, Doc,' Ben answered with a very tired smile. 'Maybe for a short while. I want to help run a business. Besides, I'm thinking that Silver Track's not the only kind of company worth investing in.'

THE END